Return to Who You Are

Return to Who You Are

One Woman's Journey to Her True Self

Miriam Minkoff

Buffalo, New York

Return to Who You Are
One Woman's Journey to Her True Self

Miriam Minkoff

First Edition

Published by
Miriam's Drum Publications
373 Colvin Ave.
Buffalo, New York 14216
www.returntowhoyouare.com

In cooperation with
RJ Communication LLC, New York

Cover photo: David Kay
Cover design: Jonathan Gullery

ISBN # 978-1-60643-851-0

Printed in the United States of America

This book is Dedicated in Loving
Memory to my Beloved Sisters ~
Bonnie McGuire
Anne Toth
&
Susan Wehle

Table of Contents

~ Preface ~

My Sexy Guardian Angel

I awoke this morning remembering a most delightful dream:

> I am at an out of town gathering waiting for my women friends to arrive. It is hot and crowded but, everyone is upbeat. I wait all day and half the night. Around midnight I give up and go to bed.
>
> My friends arrive around 3:00 am. While checking into the last room, a tall man with blonde hair arrives who needs a room as well. There are enough beds for everyone. They decide to share the room.
>
> One of my friends calls me early in the morning to tell me what happened. I bop over. She greets me at the door and walks arm and arm with me into the kitchen. Their guest is at the sink doing the dishes. His back is to us.
>
> She says, "Isn't he lovely? Maybe we could create a job for him back home." I say, "Doesn't synchronicity just blow your mind. All of you arriving at the same moment, needing a room and..."
>
> I am interrupted by this tall, lovely man's hand reaching behind and taking my right hand in his. He then pulls himself to my right side saying, "You look lovely today."
>
> He then moves ever so smoothly to my left side saying, "You know, I think I could come to your home town. There *is* something special going on here." His words shower me like delicious light butterfly kisses.

This may be one of the loveliest dreams I have ever experienced. While writing down the dream, I remember I had asked for help the night before while falling asleep.

I sat down yesterday and tried to begin writing this book at least five times throughout the the day, but nothing happened. My intentions were clear, my ideas well organized, but nothing clicked. By the end of the day I was exasperated. I gave up and went to bed. Before falling asleep I prayed for some guidance.

What intrigues me is this gorgeous blonde creature moved first to my right side and then to my left. In Judaism there is a prayer said as one is falling asleep calling the four Archangels to come first to one's right side for protection; to one's left for inspiration and creativity, in front for light in the darkness and behind for healing.

In the name of God, God of Israel,
May Michael be on my right,
On my left be Gabriel,
Uriel before me,
Behind me Raphael,
And above my head,
above my head, the Shekinah dwells. [1]

I believe I received a blessing from none other than the Archangel Gabriel that night. But, who knew archangels could be so sexy? They never mentioned that in any sacred texts. His affectionate attention gave me all the confidence I needed. I sat down that morning and started writing. I wrote for three days straight.

~ Introduction ~

I have raised five children. I have been there through earaches, stomachaches, the flu, stitches, burns...you name it. My mother was not always there for me and that sucks, but that did not stop me from *being there* for my kids. So, if I can be there for my kids no matter how much they are hurting, can I not also be there for myself?

The hurt you embrace becomes joy.
Call it into your arms where it can change. [1]
~ *Rumi*

I was raised in a German, Irish Catholic working class family in upstate New York. I graduated from college in the late 60's with a Bachelor's Degree in Dance. After graduation I lived in San Francisco, where I encountered the Dance and Poetry of the Sufi's and my spiritual life began.

I moved back East, ran a Food Co-Op and taught Sufi Dancing. A few years later I converted to Judaism, married and raised five children.

As the years passed my Jewish husband grew more religious, as I grew less. When our last two kids were preparing for college, he let me know he was tired of carrying the financial burden and felt it was my turn to pay for college.

He also let me know that my various jobs teaching music and dance throughout the city were not secure enough. He brought it up often. Eventually, I gave in. I went back to school to get a Masters Degree in Education.

It was during Student Teaching at age fifty when the shit hit the fan. I was used to being good at what I did. But in this situation, I was mediocre at best. My laid back, spontaneous approach to teaching music and dance was no match to the rigors of teaching math, reading and science on a daily basis to the same group of students. I was a fish out of water, gasping for breath.

I became increasingly anxious. A part of me knew how untrue to myself I was being. My inner turmoil grew so bad that I finally quit. Boy, what a mistake that was! That didn't help at all. In fact, it made everything ten times worse.

Overnight my anxiety mushroomed into a full blown depression. It was excruciating. My then husband, sisters, friends, kids, everyone did everything in their power to help me. During this period a friend sent me an article.

> *The sadness we experience later in life may be part of the soul's evolution. Perhaps depression is what St. John called the "Dark Night of the*

> *Soul." It is the negative forcing you to find the positive.*
>
> *In time, depression can prove to be a preparation for profound spiritual growth. This stripping away of crutches, worn out self-images and old ways of being can produce changes in one's mind that can help one ripen and attain wisdom.* [2]
>
> *~ Ram Dass*

I needed guidance badly but, was being extremely particular about whose guidance I was willing to receive. One morning while sipping coffee in my friends' home my eyes landed on Julia Cameron's *The Artist's Way*. I took it off the shelf and began leafing through it. I had found what I was looking for.

Julia's book was written with the bravado of a woman who walked her talk. She was a prolific writer who had spent the last ten years reconnecting people to the source of their creativity. There were also tons of quotes.

Her process was simple, yet profound. There were no workshops to attend and no hidden agenda or fees. I just needed to be willing to work on myself.

Julia suggests writing three pages in a journal everyday and going for a walk. That was it! It fit my needs perfectly. I could even write my grocery list if I needed to but, it had to be three pages.

Julia's style and practical wisdom taught me how to look within myself for the answers to my deepest questions. I learned to trust my intuition. In time I found my inner path. Walking my path led me on so many wondrous adventures I had to write this book.

I wish to thank Julia Cameron for being the dynamic, generous, hands-off, empowering, and immensely talented human being she is. I trust the best way for me to repay her wisdom and generosity is to *pay it forward* by sharing my journey with you. May my journey inspire you to follow your own unique path to Self, Soul and God.

Unless we are supporting the emergence
of greatness in people around us,

we are not doing our full part
to heal the world.
~ Julia Cameron

The process by which 90% of the poetry in this book came to be was neither planned nor researched. In the morning after journaling, I would simply open my books of Rumi and Hafiz and receive their poetry.

Their gifts arrived like a rose petal, lying atop my already full cup, expressing ever more poignantly the inner recesses of my heart. It is an honor and a privilege to share their wisdom.

May this book serve you

in your search for truth.

What hurts the soul most?

To live without tasting
the waters
of its own essence.
~Rumi

Return to Who You Are

~ 1 ~

Stepping Out

There is no one
in this world
that is not, longing for
God...

Everyone is trudging along
with as much dignity, courage
and style
as they possibly
can. [1]
~Hafiz

My journey began one morning in a hotel room in Myrtle Beach. Standing with my sisters far from all of our families, my older sister pulls a *Dear Abby* article out of her purse. It was from a woman describing her controlling husband.

Standing there, surrounded by my sisters' love I recognized for *the very first time* how controlling my husband had become. That morning I faced a truth I had been denying for twenty-seven years.

I have never been so frightened. I felt as though I was standing on a ledge with no where left to turn.

That afternoon we went to a sculpture garden. Our car got no further then the front gate before we saw a huge sculpture of a woman stepping out from a ledge.

Now, I have experienced my innermost thoughts *coincidently* reflected in the outside world before, known as synchronicity, but this statue was gigantic! Early the next morning, I sat down and wrote in my journal:

I am standing at the edge of an abyss. I ask myself, "What do I do now?" I remember Robert Frost's words- *The only way out is through.* I then do the scariest thing I have ever done.

I step out

God's hand appears

catching my foot.

I was utterly amazed. I had no idea what I was expecting but, it certainly was not the hand of God. Do you remember the scene in the third *Raiders of the Lost Ark* where Indiana Jones stood at the abyss? He opened his father's notebook and discovered a drawing of a person stepping out into an abyss.

When Indiana stepped from the ledge his foot landed on a stone bridge painted to look like the abyss. My abyss, on the other hand, was no parlor trick. When I stepped from the ledge I began to fall. That was the moment; God's hand swooped in and caught me.

Now, I understand this may be hard for you to believe. It is difficult for you to simply take my word for it. After giving this some thought, I realize not only is it difficult for you to take my word for it, you simply can't take my word for it.

Why is that? Because, in order for you to find out if God truly exists, you have to experience this first hand. Until you take the risk of stepping out and experience God as *being there* to catch you, you do not know for sure.

I am speaking of this not to give you
something to believe in.

I am speaking of this to show you how
you can know it for yourself. 2

~ *Echkart Tolle*

God's hand did not show up until I stepped out. Not until I was in mid-air with my heart pounding in my throat did God's hand appear. What this experience has taught me is - Each of us is the *only one* who can take that step.

I think we are all frightened
every moment
of our lives,

until

we know
Him. 4
~*Hafiz*

~ 2 ~

Finding My Fountain of Life

Why do you weep?
The source is within you. [1]
~Rumi

I had only been writing in my journal regularly for a few weeks when I had the following rather amazing experience.

> While journaling, a beautiful path through the woods appears in my mind's eye. I follow it feeling the cool earth beneath my feet and the warm sun on my face. The air is crisp and clear. The path veers left; I follow it into a meadow.
>
> There, in the center of the meadow is a magnificent water fountain glistening and gurgling in the sunlight. Its sound is so invigorating it draws me closer. I feel its vitality, sensing this fountain has an awful lot to do with me.
>
> I am so taken in by its beauty and sound, I step into its pool. Its life-giving waters rushes up my

feet, legs and torso; the sensation is wild.. Then, a delightful release, as the waters burst forth from my heart, head, eyes and fingertips, raining down all over me.

Breathing in allows me to draw the marvelous life-force in and up. Breathing out, it overflows from me to others. I feel as if I am a vessel, as if my life's work is to be a clear vessel for this magnificent, sacred life-force flowing through me.

I have a profound realization- I have found my Source. No wonder every one searches for it. But I did not find my source in Shangri-la or in any place on earth. I found my source is *within*, just like Rumi said.

Within is a place I am able to return to whenever I remember. I wish to mark my trail, like Hansel did yet, with something much more tangible. To find my way back I need to place my trust in myself and remember.

Remembrance of our dear Friend
lowers the soul's chalice
into God. [1]
~ Hafiz

I encountered my essence by following my path within. I notice that this miracle did not occur until I stopped following anyone else. It did not occur until I learned to trust and follow my own inner guidance. Why did I think following someone else's footsteps would lead me to God?

How is it that none of my religious or spiritual teachers from Catholicism, Sufism or Judaism ever said, "You know, none of us can take you to God. If you want to find God, you are going to have to trust in your intuition and follow your conscience."

My argument held up, that is, until the Dalai Lama came to town. On that auspicious day one of the very first things he said was, "You are the only one who knows the way to your soul." It was the first time I ever heard a religious/spiritual leader speak of this with such honesty.

It is frustrating to realize how few religious, spiritual teachers encourage their students to trust and follow their own inner truth and develop their own unique relationship with God.

Each of us has a way. The question we have to ask ourselves is, "What way works for me? What allows me to tune in and hear *that still small voice within?"*

What is intriguing is - each of us is the only one who knows the answer to this question. It is like stepping out from the ledge. No one else can do it for you. No one but you knows where your path is. Only you can find it.

> *The root of core self esteem is respecting the potential of each person. It involves treating each person as a separate, unique, honorable individual with rights, talents and desires* ***only that person knows.*** 3
>
> *~ Gloria Steinem*

You are the only one who knows your deepest desires. No one, myself included, knew writing daily in a journal would work for me. I simply had to put one foot in front of the other and trust. Once I did I was able to tune into my intuition, let my conscience guide me and find my authentic voice.

Not many teachers in the world
can give you as much enlightenment
in one year,

as sitting all alone, for three days,
in your closet
would
do. 4

~Hafiz

One day, not long after this, I had a surprising experience. I was journaling about the Divine Feminine when my awareness shifted. In my mind's eye I observed myself:

> Standing outside of the big closet in my parents' room in the house I grew up in. While standing there, my twelve year old self emerges from the closest. Her/my eyes are radiant with the thrill of playing hide-n-seek.
>
> This closet was the best hiding spot in the whole house. Her/my hair is a brilliant auburn. She is simply buzzing with excitement and wants me to play with her.
>
> She is *it*. Immediately she closes her eyes and counts to ten. I hide behind the long dresses in the back of the closet. I am so excited I can barely breathe.
>
> So, where does she look first? Of course she knows exactly where to find me. My spot is her spot. We step out of the closet and give each other a huge hug.
>
> During the hug I realize I have spent most of my life looking for my twelve year old. I have been looking for her ever since the day my Dad died. Then I realize, she is not the one who left. I did. I was the one who got so scared that I ran away, separating from my joyful, spontaneous, radiant self.

Years ago a rather intense rabbi named Dovid Din spoke of Adam and Eve at a Jewish Retreat. He said Adam and Eve were not cast out of the Garden of Eden. *They left*. It was their guilt and shame that separated them from the Garden of Eden.

This described exactly how I felt. I had been looking for my twelve year my whole life yet, now I realize she was not the one who was lost, I was.

The Garden of Eden still exists, as does my joyful, vibrant Self. I spent a great deal of time and energy trying to find her. Then one day, when I wasn't even trying, she simply emerged, beaming and radiant.

Do or do not.
There is no try.
~ *Yoda*

~ 3 ~

Courage to Change the Things I Can

God, grant me the Serenity
to Accept the things
I can't change.

Courage to Change
the things I Can

and Wisdom
to know
the Difference. [1]

~ *Reinhold Niebuhr*

Seven years ago I was stuck inside a very small, dank place in myself and I wanted o-u-t. After exhausting everyone's best efforts and intentions, I finally went to see to a therapist. During one of our session she asked me, "So, what do you suppose being depressed does for you?"

"Does for me?" I replied, "What the hell is

that supposed to mean?" Her question implied I had chosen to be depressed. Why in the world would I choose to do something so horrible to myself?

Besides, how could I do something like that? I am not that powerful. The question knocked around inside my head for months. Then, after one excruciatingly painful day, I finally surrendered and seriously considered an answer.

What *did* being depressed do for me? I had to admit- being depressed got me out of doing what I did not want to do. It got me out of being a regular classroom teacher. It also got me out of being controlled by my husband's money anxieties.

Answering this question changed my life dramatically. It was shocking to realize the sheer magnitude of my will. Owning up to the fact that I was powerful enough to create the mess I was in, allowed me recognize the power I had to change it.

Taking ownership of my power allowed me to draw my life-force back from the outer edges of depression, mania, powerlessness, regret and guilt. I was able to decipher the aspects of my life that were under my control from those that were not.

Emancipate yourself from mental slavery,
none but ourselves can free our minds. 2
~ *Bob Marley*

I have since reined my energy in. I am learning how to stay on top of my life-force and ride it as if I am surfing a huge wave. Sometimes it feels as if I am riding and guiding a magnificent dragon. I am happy to report I have become a much more grounded, independent, focused individual.

~

Having the *courage to change the things I can* has given me the power me to speak my truth, write this book and to ask you for your help.

Most of us recognize the peril our planet is in. But, the issue is so vast, what can we individually and collectively do to change it? Intuitively, the answer that keeps coming to mind is - apply the pragmatic principals of the *Serenity Prayer* to our relationship with our planet.

The *serenity to accept the things we can't change* means we recognize and accept what we do not have control of, like the earth's tilt. Acceptance helps us to see what; in fact we *do* have control of, which is quite a lot actually, like the intensity of hurricanes.

Becoming aware of the consequences of our actions helps us recognize the magnitude of the power we wield with every choice we make. Claiming responsibility empowers us *to change the things we can.*

> *Everyone thinks of changing the world,*
> *but, no one thinks of changing himself.*
>
> *~Tolstoy*

It is time for each of us to become much more conscious of the power inherent in our own free will.

Each personal decision affects all of us. It can contribute to the healing of the planet or to further separation, hopelessness, fear and pollution. We are responsible not only to God and to each other but also to the planet.
~ Hildegard of Bingen

Waking up and taking full responsibility for my actions, allows me to glimpse God's hand moving through mine, helping me create the world I live in. I am delighted to discover that taking responsibility for my decisions is not the burden I feared it was. Taking responsibility frees me to make better choices.

True change doesn't emerge just from action.
True change emerges from genuine understanding.

Action that flows from deep felt consciousness is action that can change the world. [4]
~Marianne Williamson

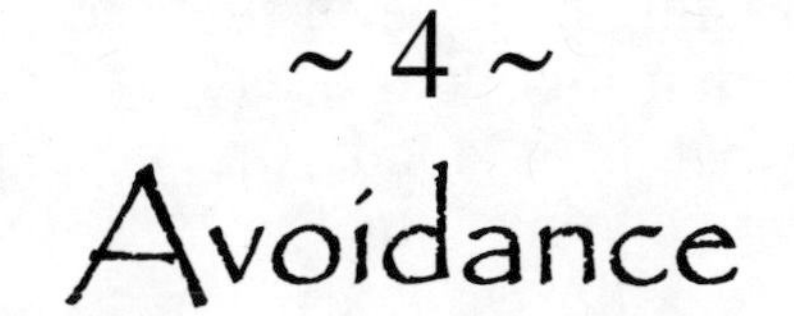

~ 4 ~
Avoidance

Soul, a moving river; *body the river bed*

Soul can break the cycle of habit and fate. [1, 2]

~ Rumi

We all know the Void. It's that empty space within we pretend we're not afraid of, but avoid like mad, the hunger we feed, that's never full; the hole we stuff that never lasts.

My Void has felt like the plant in *The Little Shop of Horrors* screaming, "Feed Me!" Yet no matter how much chocolate, alcohol, men or flirting I feed it, it demands more.

A young rabbi coined a phrase for the dance we do around the Void. It is our *A-Void-Dance.* Isn't it interesting how clever one has to be to see what is right in front of our eyes?

So, what is it about the Void we are so afraid of? Is stepping into the Void really a fate worse than death? Or does it just have a bad reputation?

I have danced around my Void most of my life. Why I even have a degree in Dance. I developed all kinds of distractions far more intriguing then stepping into my Void.

Come to think of it, this is what addictions are. Addictions are the distractions we come up with to avoid taking the next step. They are the *monkeys on the side of the road* we find far more entertaining than the truth that needs facing.

Any search moves away from the spot
where the object of the quest is...

Listen to the sound of waves within you.
There you are, dreaming your thirst.

When the water you want
is inside

the big vein
in your neck.
~ Rumi

I can say with all honesty that the Void isn't really so bad. It's the *anticipation* of facing the Void that can kill ya. Dr. Seuss does a terrific job describing the hell our a-void-dance puts us through in his book, *I Had Some Trouble on the Way to Solla Sollew.* In it a young yellow creature leaves his troubles behind and sets forth for:

> *Solla Sollew, on the banks of the beautiful river Wah-Hoo.*
>
> *Where they never have troubles!*
> *At least very few.*
>
> *~ Dr. Seuss*

After many trials and tribulations our yellow friend arrives in Solla Sollew only to discover the gate into Solla Sollew is locked. When who should come by but, a chap on his way to *Bella Bu-Ball, where they never have troubles, no troubles at all!*

Our yellow friend is tempted to follow, but then he changes his mind and decides to go home. He buys a big bat and lets *his troubles have trouble with him.*

This is, what I finally did. It happened the night I admitted what being depressed *did* for me. After realizing *I had chosen* to run away from my life, I sat down on my front porch, got out my journal and turned to face the fears that had been stalking me.

> They look like Darth Vader and Tibetan Death masks. A chapter from the novel *Tales of Dalai Lama* by Pierre

Delattre comes to mind.

The Dalai Lama is awakened early in the morning by the monks in charge of his training. They place him in a room lined with Tibetan Death masks. The young lama sees the terrifying masks and faints on the spot.

The monks drag the young lama out and return the next morning. They place him in the room again. The lama remains conscious for a moment before fainting. Then the day arrives when the Dalai Lama could remain all day in the room with the masks. 4

I faced my fears that night and I did not die. I walked the razor thin edge of truth through the Dark Night of my Soul and into the light of day. The further I walked, the wider the edge of truth became, until one day that truth became the very ground of my being.

Today like every other day
we wake up empty and frightened.

Don't go to the door of the study
and begin reading.

Take down the dulcimer.

Let the beauty you love
be what you do.

There are hundreds of ways to kneel
and kiss the ground.

~ Rumi

~ 5 ~

Hiding in Plain Sight

We are all on a quest. A quest requiring knights to become, princesses to rescue, bad knights to triumph over, dragons to slay, love to be true for and a truth to die for. It involves a sacred duty, a moral compass, chivalry and honor.

The story of King Arthur and his Knights of the Round Table reflect our inner quest perfectly. One approach to dream interpretation says we are everyone in our dream. This same principal holds true for archetypal myths.

This means we are King Arthur, Lady Guinevere, Sir Lancelot and Morgane, Arthur's wicked half sister. We are the noble Sir Gawain, as well as the dark knights that challenge him. This also means we are Parsifal, the gentle knight the Grail King asks to find and return the Holy Grail.

What is the Holy Grail? What does it represent? What purpose does it serve? When I found my inner fountain, I realized my fountain was a Sacred Vessel that allowed me to contain my very Essence. My inner fountain is my Holy Grail.

What one's Holy Grail contains is even more significant than the Grail itself. For the Holy Grail contains our very souls. Each of us has a Holy Grail containing our Essence. Each of us is the Holy Grail hiding in plain sight.

I can be aware I contain the very Essence of Life, if and when I am brave and humble enough to walk up and taste it. To have such an adventure we *don't even need to leave our room.* There are moments when the bravest thing we can do is - look within.

You don't need to leave your room.
Remain sitting at your table and listen.
Don't even listen, simply wait.
Don't even wait.
Be quite still and solitary.
The world will freely offer itself to you.
To be unmasked it has no choice.
It will roll in ecstasy at your feet.
~ *Franz Kafka*

But how do we learn to see with new eyes? Writing is what helps me. It is not my strong suit but it keeps me honest. Writing helps me stay *on my thread* and weave my story together.

Please remember that we are the dark element woven into the stories as well, the dark knight *and* Sir Gawain, the Wicked Witch and Glinda, Darth Vader and Yoda. This is significant. For myths and stories are one of the few places we let our guard down enough to actually relate and learn from our darker nature.

We are the imperfect ones and those worthy of finding the Holy Grail. It is our dark natures that need to be triumphed. We are the dragon and the one who learns how to direct its fiery energy and passion. It is our fears that need to be conquered and our hearts that need opening.

In order to begin our quest, we need to leave our home just as Frodo, Dorothy and Luke Skywalker did. In order to appreciate how profoundly beautiful the life we have actually is, we need to be tested within an inch of our lives.

The journey of a thousand miles
begins with but a single step.
~ *Confucius*

Why else would *Star Wars, the Wizard of Oz and King Arthur and the Knights of the Roundtable* be so near and dear to our hearts? The archetypal imagery they evoke resonates with our quest.

Writers tap into their own inner quest to write an archetypal myth. The more truthful they are with themselves, the more it resonates with our inner truth. This is one of the more profound ways we can be of service one another.

My intention in writing this book is to encourage you to trust your intuition, listen to your conscience, discover your authentic voice and let your inner compass guide you to the Home of Your Soul.

For you are the *only one* who knows where your soul is. You are the only one who knows where you've hidden your treasure. Many cultures tell the story of finding one's treasure. This one is a Nasruddin story. One night Nasruddin was down on his hands and knees looking for his keys under a street light.

"So where did you last see them?" asks his student. "Oh, I lost them at home," replied the teacher. "If you lost them at home why are we looking for them out here?" "Because, "Nasruddin replied, "this is where the light is."

Isn't this what most of us do? We search for our treasure in the street or under a bridge when our treasure is waiting to be found where we left it, within our own hearts.

A friend once shared an insight on the Wizard of Oz saying, each of the characters already possessed the qualities they sought from the Wizard. The Scarecrow was the brains of the operation. It was the Lion who stormed the Witches castle and it was the Tin Man who kept bursting into tears. Each one of us, just as each of them, seeks that which we already are.

~ 6 ~

The Love of Power or The Power of Love

There are two types of power. One is Power Over; the other is Power Within. Power Over shows up as control and dominance. Power Within demonstrates itself as empowerment of Self and others. The Power Over paradigm has permeated our consciousness and our culture for millennia. It is one of the reasons our planet is in such peril today.

Power over others is weakness
disguised as strength.
True power is within. [1]
~ Eckhart Tolle

An essay written by Irene Claremont de Castillejo, a female Jungian analyst helped me understand Power Within. I first read Irene's work over twenty five years ago. Yet, her insights continue to inform my decision making to this day.

> *I like to think of every person being linked to God by an invisible thread. A thread that is unique for each of us, a thread that can never be broken or taken away, but can elude us.*
>
> *Being on one's thread is being in touch with the Self. This means knowing what one knows and standing firmly on the ground of one's own inner truth. Life seems to happen more fully around us when we are on our thread.*
>
> *Paying attention to being on one's thread should not be mistaken for egotism. It is in fact, the opposite of egoism. Being on one's thread means not trying to exert influence or have power over others at all. Trying to change other people's thoughts or actions leads one away from being on one's thread.* [2]
>
> *~ Irene Claremont de Castillejo*

Setting others free from my dominance allows for something more than my ego to enter the room. The more I can *get out of my own way*, the more I am able to pull my ego back and witness the miracle of life unfolding before my eyes, without me interfering. Or should that be spelled inter*fear*ing?

The more I stop trying so hard to control everything, the more the universe is able to swoop in and offer a multitude of much more interesting possibilities.

Freeing others from my dominance also affords me more time to *tend my own vital thread*. When we truly focus on fulfilling our life's work, we no longer have the time or the desire to occupy ourselves with controlling the lives of others, freeing them to fulfill their own life's work.

~

Yesterday I saw a license plate that read, *Do Now*. It reminded me to loosen the reins I have on life and simply allow the present moment to be.

If the creative possibilities life has to offer are so lovely, why do I struggle with them so? Why do I have such a hard time letting the universe surprise me? If Power Over takes so much of my time, effort and energy, why do I keep choosing to invest in it?

Power Over hides our light, erecting a mask we try desperately to make others believe we are. No matter how hard we try, the truth inevitably shows up and does us the favor of kicking our mask loose. Although the pain can be excruciating, it is worth every second of not getting away with our bullshit a moment longer.

The truth had to kick me pretty hard to get my mask off. I was down for the count for ten months solid. Yet in time, this one and the same truth became the catalyst that helped me arise from the ashes like a phoenix.

To celebrate my ascent and transformation my hairdresser and I decided to stop dyeing my hair. I have since let white hair shine.

The truth comes along and opens the curtain on us, just as Toto did to the Wizard of Oz, revealing just how much time, energy and effort most of us invest in keeping our mask in place.

"Pay no attention to that man behind the curtain." The wizard says. But isn't our real selves *that man behind the curtain?* Wasn't it not being paid attention to that caused us to puff up our egos in the first place? We spend so much of our time energy portraying the false images of ourselves that we hardly have any energy left for our real selves.

Be Yourself.
It requires too much effort
to be anything else.
~ Anonymous

When I looked behind my curtain what I discovered was, I was trying way too hard to be someone other than who I am. This was a significant first step. A friend once shared, "You can never become who you want to be until you stop trying to be who you are not." Then I discovered how Carl Rogers phrased it.

The curious paradox is that when I accept
myself just as I am, then I can change.
~ Carl Rogers

Not working 24/7 to impress everyone I meet allows for something beside my ego to come forth. I have to ask myself, "Can I let go? Can I take the chance to see if something beyond my ego actually exists?

What is it my ego is so terribly afraid of?" After sincerely asking myself this question, I discover what I am most afraid of. I worry if I am worthy of receiving all the love I want and need.

~

One New Years Weekend I taught a movement workshop at The Phoenicia Pathwork Center on Body Splits:

> We begin by exploring the difference between the front and back halves of our bodies, noticing how much energy we invest in our front.
>
> I am moving around the room with a blue cape draped across my arms. My front is able to produce whatever anyone wants or needs from my magical blue cape. While moving toward the back of this magnificent space, I begin to see through the veneer of my front.
>
> Suddenly the weight of the cape becomes so heavy I can barely hold it up. A scene from Kazanzakas' novel *Francis* comes to mind. In it the narrator and St. Francis are walking down a road. Lying on the side of the road is a beggar. Francis walks over and picks up the beggar, carrying him in his arms with great tenderness and love. Slowly the beggar in Francis's arms transforms into Christ.
>
> I then understand that I have been denying my brokenness. I now feel the weight of the cape for what it is my woundedness. In the sanctity of this sacred space I accept the love of St. Francis and carry my wounded self with more love and compassion than ever before.

Kazanzakas' story of Francis demonstrates how transformative the power of love is. Learning to have compassion for my woundedness allowed me to accept and love myself as I am. The love and support I felt that day continues to give me the strength and courage to move away from Power Over and toward Power Within.

There is a shift in awareness occurring. Many of us are moving toward being true to Power Within and moving away from Power Over.

> There are moments when I feel like Richard Dreyfuss sculpting his mashed potatoes in *Close Encounters of the Third Kind.* I am responding to the profound call coming from within and I don't believe I am the only one hearing this call.
>
> There is a shift occurring of monumental proportions called a **Paradigm Shift.** We are independently and collectively choosing to shift away from the Love of Power toward the Power of Love.

When the Power of Love overcomes
the Love of Power, the world
will know Peace.

~ Jimi Hendrix

Responding to one's vulnerability and pain with empathy and compassion is perceived from a Jungian perspective, as a feminine response. Each of us carries both masculine and feminine qualities.

In Jungian Psychology our masculine aspects are understood as the line, rational knowledge, analysis, expansion, self assertion and as Yang. Our feminine aspects are recognized as the circle, intuitive knowledge, synthesis, contraction, integration and as Yin.

Our masculine and feminine aspects respond differently to vulnerability and pain. When we are in an emergency, we need to be focused, rational, direct and detached from our pain and vulnerability. This is perceived as a masculine response.

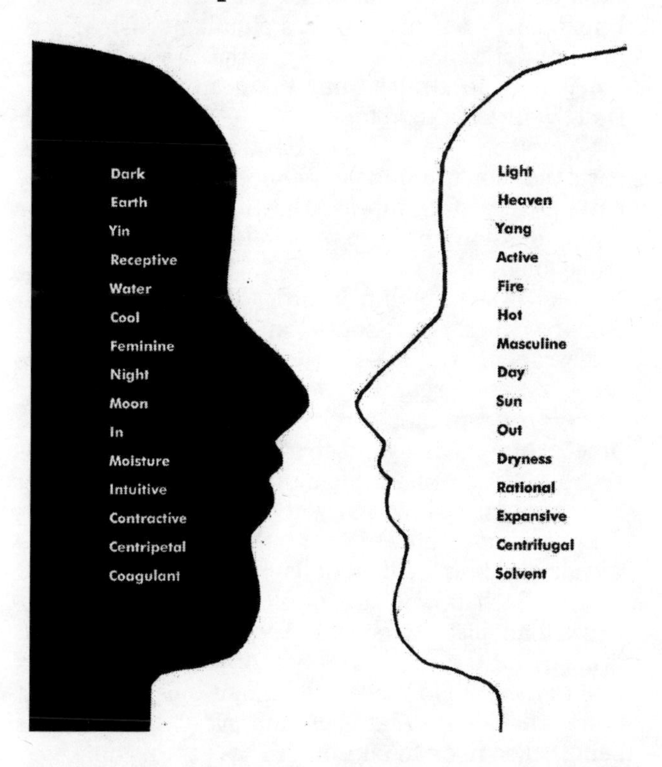

We can only place our vulnerability and pain on hold for so long. Eventually our needs have to be addressed and tended to. This requires a very different set of skills. Skills such as empathy, compassion and acceptance are needed. These are perceived as feminine.

In the midst of trying to explain the aspects of one's psyche as concretely as possible, my awareness makes a dramatic shift.

A loud voice suddenly begins speaking to me from within: I am the circle, not the line. I am the God within everyone and everything. I am the Immanent. I am in all places simultaneously. I am the Omnipresence and I am not the Deserving One. You'll have to stretch your brain around this one. Don't worry, it's good for you.

I am the rejected, dark aspects of you, the parts that don't fit into your concept of God, but these parts don't just disappear. They linger, crying out for love and attention. I can only hold onto them for you for so long.

At some point, in order to be at peace with your own heart and soul, you need to redeem and forgive them. You need to bring them up and out of the darkness I represent and into the light of your being. You are not forgiving me. You are in the process of forgiving yourselves.

All of you, at this moment in time, are being given a great task. When you bring forth your truths from the very depths of your being, bring them all the way up and into the light of day.

Each of you are fulfilling a sacred task for more than just yourselves. You are being asked to bring about the transformation of your very souls, as well as the transformation of human consciousness. It is no coincidence that each and every one of you is being called upon to take on this task at this time.

We know it isn't easy, but you need to trust your hearts and your deepest connection to God in order to allow US to come through. You need to be courageous, independent and unafraid. You will also need to give people time to adjust to this idea. They may freak at first. It is only natural. Don't take it personally.

Back to my own voice: Yes, the Feminine aspect of God is coming. She is coming to reunite with Her Beloved, restoring sexuality to spirituality, allowing us to reconnect to our own source, restoring equilibrium on a physical, emotional, intellectual and spiritual level.

We won't need nearly as much stuff to feel whole, complete. We'll find lovelier and more direct ways of meeting our needs, allowing us to shift from *having more to being more*, which is what our planet needs to survive.

The voice that just came through reminds me of a Gnostic writing called *Thunder Perfect Mind*. It was found in 1945 by a peasant in three feet high earthen jars with thirteen papyrus books in Upper Egypt. They were published in *The Gnostic Gospels* written by Elaine Pagels.

Scholars agree, the texts discovered at Nag Hammadi were written by Early Christians in 350-400 A.D. One of the more extraordinary texts, entitled *Thunder Perfect Mind*, is a poem spoken in the voice of the Divine Feminine.

I am the first and the last.
I am the honored and the scorned one.
I am the whore and the holy one.
I am the wife and the virgin...
I am the barren one and many are my sons...
I am knowledge, and ignorance...
I am shameless; I am ashamed...
I am strength, and I am fear...
I am foolish, and I am wise...
I am godless, I am one whose God is great. [3]

~ Thunder Perfect Mind
Nag Hammadi

I wonder why I, and most of us, have been taught to not trust a voice such as this, a voice that was buried both literally and figuratively for over fifteen hundred years!

Do we not trust this inner voice because of what was done to the women who heard such voices in the past? I ask you with all honesty, “Was there anything I said that was so terrible? If not, why such fear, such utter disdain?”

Or is it because *Thunder Perfect Mind* and I speak from the feminine voice held in contempt by Patriarchy? This contempt is how Patriarchy holds the feminine in its shadow.

Not listening to our own inner voice may well be one the ways each of continues to suppress our own inner feminine. Is not trusting our authentic voice how we unconsciously hold back the emergence of the Divine Feminine? If that is the case, the very best thing each of us can do is tune into our truest sense of self and listen closely.

There is one thing stronger
than all the armies in the world.

And that is an idea whose
time has come.
~ Victor Hugo

~ 7 ~

Fixing What's Broken
Tikkun Olam

Feminine Masculine

This morning while attempting to repair my favorite wine glass, I am blown away by how perfectly the two halves symbolize the feminine and masculine aspects of our psyche. The graceful receptive feminine cup is turned down toward the earth, whiles the masculine base and stem are in an eternal pursuit upward.

As I set the cup of the feminine down over the masculine stem, the energy feels self sufficient but trapped. It feels as if the masculine is wrapping himself up inside a burkah, using the feminine to feel safe, using all of the feminine energy for himself.

Turning the cup up with the base inside, feels just as self serving as the one above. Only this time it is the feminine focusing only on what she can get, keep and have for herself.

I then apply the Gorilla glue, hold the cup on top of the stem and count to ten. By the time I get to four I am flooded by the sense of a return to wholeness.

Once the receptive cup of the feminine is placed atop the directive stem of the masculine, it feels as if everything has been returned to its proper place.

Suddenly, the energy that was jammed up inside the stem is freed to fill the cup to overflowing, allowing even more energy to flow in. I sense a Return to Oneness, as if a precious piece that was lost has been returned.

It feels like I am riding waves of a joyous reunion. The authenticity is so honest and real, it is disarming. I hear a resounding "Yes!" called out from the depth of my being. "This is real." This is how truth works. It rings true.

The moment I reconnect the stem and cup it feels like I have slipped into place the last two pieces of a huge jig saw puzzle. The moment they slide into place, they disappear, revealing the whole picture instead of its parts. The whole *is* greater than the sum of its parts.

Their reunion reconnects the very fabric of life. In Judaism this is known as Tikkun Olum, Fixing the World,

Repairing my inner chalice, allows me to realign with my own inner truth, helping me remember my way back to the very Waters of Life; back to where the emptier I am, the fuller I can become.

What if the Holy Grail is not lost but, it is broken? Glancing over I see the bottom half of the cup, lying on its side. It looks like a child's pacifier. Talk about a lousy substitute for the Feminine!

I keep pretending to be satisfied with broken half truths, trying to derive nourishment from an insufficient reality. No wonder I have addictions. A part of me knows something is missing. I sense there is a whole truth that is not being brought forth.

If you bring forth what is within you,
what you bring forth will heal you.

If you do not bring forth what is within you,
what you do not bring forth will destroy you. [1]
~ Jesus, Gospel of
St. Thomas

My gut senses a lie has been rolling around inside Christianity for millennia, an irritating grain of sand that simply will not go away. I sense there is a truth of mammoth proportions the Catholic Church does not want me to know. But look, the grain of sand has turned into a pearl of wisdom ready to be honored and recognized.

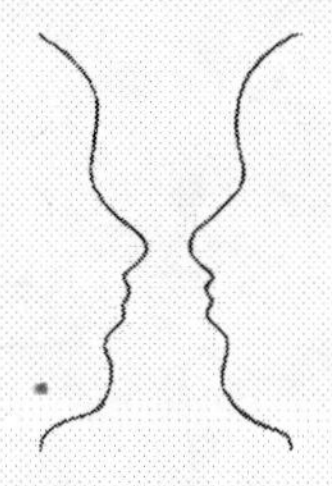

Returning the feminine to her place of honor restores a sacred balance within me, bringing about a Sacred Equilibrium, a Return to Oneness and Wholeness.

I looked for and found this sacred union in other religions. Yet the truth I found there did not repair my chalice. I have to return to the source of my brokenness to repair my chalice. I have to return to my Catholic roots to fix what is broken.

I am standing on the sacred red earth beneath a Catholic Church. I recognize the red earth from of my dream. I am bringing forth this sacred truth on the ground of my being.

> I am returning Mary Magdalene to her rightful place alongside her beloved, Jesus. I am saying this out loud and in print. I have been wrestling with bringing forth my entire adult life. Amen. So Be It.

Why was the whole truth of Mary Magdalene not brought forth? Would St. Peter have changed the basic tenants of Christianity because he was jealous of Jesus loving Mary Magdalene more then him? *The Gospel of Mary Magdalene* suggests this to be so. 2

After bringing this forth I look out my window and see a shimmering golden cross of light streaming right toward me. I feel welcomed home within the open, loving arms and heart of God.

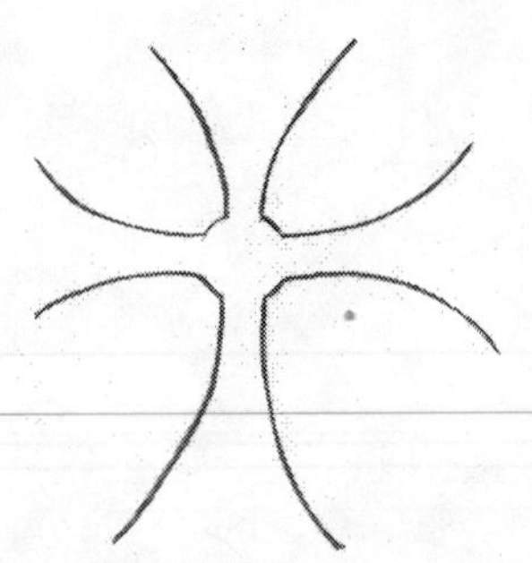

Replacing the rejected cornerstone of Mary Magdalene allows me to see and accept my Catholicism and Christianity on my own terms. I am finally finding peace within the religion I was raised in. Returning Mary Magdalene to her rightful place restores my sense of balance within and without, symbolized as an Open Heart Centered Cross, Sacred Balance and Individuation.

~ 8 ~

Interfacing

Years ago, in the midst of preparing for my son's Bar Mitzvah, I went to a Rites of Passage Symposium in my State Capital. The night before the symposium I had the following dreams.

> I am visiting an old friend who lives in the country. We are walking through the woods to see a project his son has just completed. We enter a cabin and there, in the corner of the cabin, is a solid beautifully built hearth. Carved into the keystone of the arch is, "To Mom, love Jacob." The young man in this dream, as in real life, is a conscious, spiritually awakened soul.
>
> In the second dream I am riding in the passenger seat of a car being driven by a crazed young man. He is using the car to gouge deep ruts into meadows. He is literally tearing up the countryside with his car. It seems as if he is trying to destroy everything he can get his hands on.
>
> He then turns to me saying, "Give some oxygen to my mother. She's in the back seat!" I turn and look in the back seat and sure enough, there she is, along with a tank of oxygen stuck between the seats. He

> tells me to peel back the duct tape covering her mouth, so I can periodically give her oxygen through a small hose!

These dreams have stayed with me for many years. Acknowledging that everyone in the dream is me places the second dream much more squarely in my lap.

> There are moments when I can tune in and sense my destructive one. I can feel his sense of rejection and abandonment. I also sense how frightened and alone he is fending for himself all this time. I do not believe he has any idea how destructive he is. I think he is destroying things simply to feel something, anything.

I have always had a lot of physical energy. There were many times when I had no idea what to do with all my energy. When I lived in the country in my twenties, a friend and I were the chainsaw ladies. In college I majored in Dance, preferring African, Brazilian and Modern Dance to Ballet. As I got older, I redirected my dance energy into African drumming.

I realized that cutting down trees, dancing and drumming were constructive ways for me to direct what could become destructive energy.

The different nature of the two young men reminds me of the story of Jacob and Esau. As the story goes Jacob and his mother Rachel, trick Isaac, the Patriarch into giving his blessing to the more spiritual yet younger son Jacob. By the time Esau, the coarser, more earth-bound older son discovers what has happened, it is too late. The blessing has already been given.

The question then arises, “What happens to the coarser son?” He doesn’t just disappear.

> While writing this, I slip inside the dream, I sense the young man who built the hearth as constantly striving upward, whereas the more tragic youth, is constantly looking down.

> I wonder what would happen if my two young men where to change their point of view. What if the one who is always looking upward were to turn and look down? If he did, he would see someone who looks just like him standing there. Isn’t he just narcissistic enough to want to know who that is?
>
> I then sense the earth-bound youth feeling someone looking down at him. He instinctively turns and looks up to see who it is. I hear the skyward youth saying, “This is hard. I keep trying to get out of here, but no matter where I go, here I am. Hey, wait a minute. That guy looks just like me. Whoa! I feel nauseous and woozy. Look out! I’m falling.”

Meanwhile, the earth-bound youth looks up and sees someone falling down out of the sky. He catches the skyward youth and sets his feet on the ground next to him.

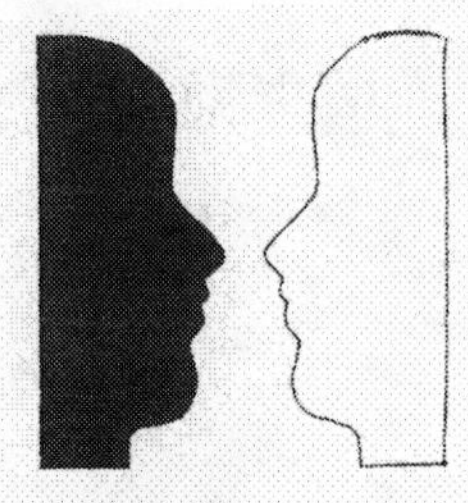

Standing there, the two young men recognize a part of themselves they have been out of touch with for a very long time. The tension between them slackens.

Suddenly, I feel like Alice tumbling down the hole toward Wonderland, vulnerable and exposed. It feels as though I am dropping through an invisible fence. I feel as if I am falling and I haven't landed anywhere yet.

I am shocked by how dramatic the effects are. I realize now how ungrounded my spiritual youth is and how much he needs his grounded brother. With my spiritual one in freefall, I was nauseous, out of control and very vulnerable. Yet, it was not a totally uncomfortable sensation.

The next morning, still disoriented, I went to work. What unfolded around me that day was fascinating. Everyone was much more at ease then usual. The kids, staff and I created some great rhymes, rhythms and raps together.

I was relaxed, creative and had fun all day long. The feedback I received from both students and staff was, "Yeah, whatever it is you're doing, keep doing it." My not having it completely together was a welcome relief to everyone, including myself. I gotta get out of my way more often.

There's a difference between knowing the path and walking the path.
~ The Matrix

The Lens of Duality

Most of us unconsciously accept the tension duality generates within our lives. Yet, working with this dream helps me realize I have a choice. I do not have to live an either/or existence.

I no longer have to see things as good *or* bad, high or low, light or dark, right or wrong. It is divisive, destructive and *it ain't necessarily so.*

Besides, viewing life through the lens of duality is only one way of perceiving the world. Learning to look at life from a different point of view may be uncomfortable at first but, it has its advantages.

When my two young men faced each other, I felt a shift. This shift created an opportunity in me that never existed before. In *Coming to Our Senses* Dr. Morris Berman perceives this as an opportunity, saying it is as analogous to a crab that has shed its old shell and has not formed a new one yet.

Dr. Berman suggests staying with the uncomfortable sensations and not rushing to forming a new shell yet. He proposes *staying in the process*.

He goes on to state that many of us seek *peace* in order to escape from *freedom,* describing the sense of order and being right our –isms give us: whether our -ism is Feminism, Communism, Racism, Veganism, Capitalism, Catholicism, or Zionism.

He recommends trading in one's old hard thick shell for a lighter, more flexible one, encouraging us to give up the comfort of being *right,* for the uncomfortableness of *freedom*.

> *No one can learn this for us. No matter how we may search outside ourselves for he or she who will save us from the* ***burden of our freedom,*** *if the message we find is authentic, it will send us right back to ourselves.* [1]
>
> *~ Jean-Yves Leloup*

When asked how does one we stay in the process? Morris Berman suggests:

Live with the question until
an answer emerges.

When the answer comes,
it emerges from a true, authentic base. [2]
~ Morris Berman

I have only recently discovered it was Rainer Maria Rilke who originally posed this thought in his *Letters to A Young Poet.*

> *Have patience with everything unresolved in your heart; try to love the questions themselves, as if they were locked rooms or books written in a foreign language.*
>
> *Don't search for the answers, which could not be given to you now, because you would not be able to live them. And the point is to live everything. Live the questions now. Perhaps then, someday far in the future, you will gradually, without even noticing it, live your way into the answer.* 3
>
> *~ Rainer Maria Rilke*

Isn't this how one develops one's philosophy of life? Their wisdom has proven to be the best advice I have received for finding the answers to my fiercest questions.

This is the reason writing has become such a portal to my soul. Writing lets my thoughts simmer, allowing me to return to stir the pot until it tastes just right.

~

I have recently discovered the astonishing book *Conversations with God* written by Neale Walsch. In one section Neale asks God, "How do you answer my questions?" God replies:

> *Go ahead. Ask me anything... The whole universe will I use to bring*

you the answer. So be on the lookout. You may ask me a question. Then put this book down. But watch. Listen.

The words in the next song you hear. The information in the next article you read. The story line of the next movie you watch. The chance utterance of the next person you meet. Or the whisper of the next river, ocean, breeze that caresses your ear - all these are Mine.

I will speak to you, if you will listen. I will come to you, if you will invite Me. I will show you then that I am always here, always. 4

~ *God to Neale Walsch*

God speaks to us when we are hurting and do not know what to do next. My angel did not show up when I began writing this book until I asked.

We are finally able to hear because our egos and defensiveness are no longer blocking our ability to receive Life's messages. We are able to hear because we are finally willing to listen. It is here in those uncomfortable tight places that the universe swoops in telling us exactly what we need to hear, in a way that we can hear it.

Returning to the young men from the dream, I recognize just how badly my spiritual youth needs his grounded brother. Being undervalued and unrecognized had everything to do with his hopelessness.

This is a perfect example of what Jungians call the shadow. Not appreciating the value or worth of my grounded one is what caused his desperation and destructiveness.

Discovering he has a purpose gives him reason to live and perhaps, to be loved. Poet Robert Bly once described the shadow as *the long black bag we drag behind us*:

> *We all come into this world as a three hundred and sixty degree personality, a trailing blaze of glory. Soon we discover there are aspects of ourselves our parents and family don't like. So we stuff them into a long black bag we drag behind us.*
>
> *We spend the first eighteen years of our lives stuffing different aspects of ourselves into that bag and the rest of our lives taking them out.* [5]
>
> *~ Robert Bly*

Discovering one's purpose in life sustains all of us. The tension between my two young men has improved dynamically. I no longer have to choose between the spiritual or the earth-bound aspect of myself. I need them both. Their coming together creates a whole greater than the sum of its parts. I need my light and dark aspects to be a sane, embodied whole.

Now is the time for you to know
that all you do is sacred.

Why not consider a lasting
truce with yourself and God.

Now is the time to understand
that all your ideas of right and wrong

where just a child's training wheels
to be laid aside.

Now is the time when you can finally live

with veracity (truth)
and love. 6
~ Hafiz

I am re-wiring myself, replacing the old rigid wires of right *or* wrong, good or bad, spiritual or sexual with these cool fiber optic ones. They are supple *and* strong, flexible and resilient. They are woven with the love and struggle of honoring all that I am.

You don't have to be good.

You don't have to walk through the desert for a thousand miles on your knees repentant.

You only have to let the soft animal of your body love what it loves.
~ Mary Oliver

~

In education circles there are numerous studies on what makes certain students succeed where others fail. What supports their success? One of the qualities successful students possess is called an Internal Locus (Focus) of Control. They somehow understand how to control themselves from within.

Their internal control demonstrates itself as

self-discipline, attentiveness, self-organization, as well as the ability to concentrate, focus and set attainable goals.

Students who lack this internal order have more trouble controlling their behavior. They end up unconsciously seeking others to control their behavior for them. This is known as an External Locus of Control.

The question then becomes how do we empower ourselves and others to shift from thinking we need an External Locus and discover our own Internal Locus of Control? How do we help ourselves and others gain the respect, freedom, independence we need and desire?

The movie *The Golden Compass* expresses the power of discovering one's internal compass beautifully. In it a young girl uses her golden compass to discover her truth and be of service to her friends, her family and the world. Yet in order to access her compass, the girl has to be alone. Giving ourselves permission to be alone is something I believe many of us could do more often.

I never knew how un- lonely,
being alone could be.
~ Ellen Burstyn

Last night I had two dreams.

> In the first I am walking in the rain at night with a man named Earth. we talk about drumming as we walk down a valley, cross a creek and climb up a hill to where his cabin is neatly tucked into the side.

> The door of his cabin opens. We are greeted by the warmth and comfort of a fire burning in the fireplace. A friend of mine named Eric is there. We are surprised to see one another.
>
> In the second dream I am driving a motorcycle, boat or something fast, dangerous and exhilarating to ride! Standing next to it in a gas station I think, "Maybe I should wear a helmet." A group of women are standing nearby. I ask them what they think. They suggest I wear a helmet and paint the helmet white on the front and black in the back.
>
> There's my clue. My hair is white and the back is dark. This vehicle of intense energy I am learning to ride/fly has everything to do with my head. I am learning to get comfortable riding the energy of my intellect.

Now if everyone in my dream is me, then I am Earth living in a cabin in a dark, moist valley near a river. I am also Eric, who is in real life a grounded, handsome, caring excellent saxophone player married to a kind and beautiful woman.

In the second dream I am learning how to ride the intense, dynamic energy of my intellect. My women friends admire the energy but, remind me to stay connected to the dark, feminine Yin energy in the back of my head. This reminder helps me relax and stay on top of my newly realized Yang, masculine life-force. Getting in touch with my intellect is both exhilarating and terrifying.

My internal Eric represents an inner masculine living harmoniously in a cabin on the side of the hill in the valley of the feminine. This strikes me as Yang living in Yin and loving every second of it. Both inner and outer Eric's love for life and music has allowed him to cultivate an appreciation for the feminine by following his heart and his art.

~

I need to pause for a moment to reflect on regret. When I was depressed and in the depths of despair, I experienced profound regret. I realized that if I did not change I would live the rest of my life with intense regret. The thought was utterly terrifying.

At the time I did not believe I had the necessary courage or will power to change my life one iota, making these the darkest moments of all. Yet I recall how strongly I desired to no longer live this way. Looking back, I realize now that that was my turning point.

The resolve of my decision to no longer live with regret gave me the courage I needed to break through my fear and resistance. This inner resolve provided the ground I walked on as I walked away from my marriage. During this transition phase a quote showed up:

It is never too late to be who you might have been.
It is never too late to be who you truly are.
~ George Eliot

The day after the Earth dream I went for a walk around the lake in my local park, trying to resolve the internal images of Earth, Eric and the powerful, iridescent energies that were stuck in my head. Half way around the lake, the saying of an old Sufi teacher came to mind:

Thinking will get you more stinking
than drinking but, to feel is for real. 7
~ *Rev Joe Miller*

I was ill at ease with how to stay on top of my masculine, motorcycle energy, compared to how grateful and at ease my inner masculine was with the feminine. I thought, "If I could just drop into my body and trust it more, I would be able to ride its waves of energy without falling off."

Within a millisecond I saw two birds over the lake. I look- no flapping wings; it must be hawks, and indeed it was! The outlines of their bodies appeared where the water met the sky. At first glance the hawks' wings appeared to be the lips of heaven and earth kissing.

> I watch the hawks drop the weight of their bodies onto the air currents, allowing the spirals of air to carry them higher and higher. It reminds me of

the first time I learned how to body surf. Only the hawks are riding on waves of air!

Then three more hawks arrive. While standing there amazed, two more hawks join, then three more! It appears to be the most natural thing in the world. Meanwhile, there are *ten* hawks dipping, diving and spiraling over the lake in the middle of the city. It is a breathtakingly beautiful sight to behold.

Time passes and the hawks eventually fly away. I walk further around the lake. Then one hawk returns. She is soaring above my head in gorgeous spirals for what feels like an eternity. I watch closely, thinking, "Holy Shit, this hawk is giving me a one on one flying lesson on how to ride air currents!"

My eyes follow her as she drops the entire weight of her body onto the current of air and then, she lets go, riding a spiraling current of air up, up, up and away.

The next morning I record in my journal what I thought I heard her say:

I am not anything you need to try for.

We are already one.

Sometimes you see it. Sometimes you don't.
You keep trying to get to where you already are.

Drop the struggle.
Step out of the two into the one.
Shift your focus.

You don't have to do anything.

Be who you already are.
Be who you already are.

~ your hawk

I was so taken by this experience that it took me a while to realize just how miraculous the whole encounter was. Somehow, the ten hawks over the lake and my own personal flying instructor seemed altogether natural. It was not until the next morning when I began to journal about it all that it hit me. If I hadn't taken the time to stop and reflect, this miracle could have slipped right past me.

Miracles seem to arrive when we do not know what to do next and sincerely ask for guidance, just like Neale Walsch and God said. I am utterly grateful.

> *The unconscious helps us by informing us of things which by all logic we could not possibly know. Consider if you will, synchronistic phenomena, premonitions and dreams that come true.* 8
>
> ~ *C. G. Jung*

I see Eric living in the cabin with the fireplace burning nestled on the side of the dark, wet mountain as the white eye of Yang in the dark home of the Yin.

My women friends reminding me to let my dark, feminine nature guide me as I ride my fabulous motorcycle of masculine energy, I see as the dark eye of Yin riding the energy of Yang.

Isn't that cool? I never understood the Yin Yang symbol so viscerally before. This is not a solution to a problem. This is a whole new way to envision the dance of life going on within me.

My solution between my two young men resolved a great deal of tension. Yet, over time, *living the question* is what helped me *live my way into the answer*. *Living the question* allowed me to receive very personal guidance on how to live the Tao, as well as, a more authentic life.

~9~

Reverberation

Recently, I released emotions I had been carrying around for over thirty years. It all started the day my daughter went back to college for her junior year.

She had been home for the entire summer without a job. So when I say it was time for her to go back to school, *it was time for her to go back to school.* About a half hour after she left, I found myself on the verge of tears. Not knowing what else to do, I sat down and started to journal.

Feelings I had buried long ago slowly began rising to the surface. The more I wrote, the stronger the emotional waves came crashing through. I was sobbing, but still had no idea why. Then it hit me. My mother died when I went away to college in my junior year.

I was living on my own for the first time when I received the news. I rushed home and attended her funeral. I was so busy *becoming independent* that I did not take the time I needed to feel, let alone grieve her death.

What is especially sad is that my mother and I had just started getting along again. Her death was a great shock. Instead of taking the time to feel and go through my many conflicting emotions, I wrapped them up and stashed them away so I could rush back to college. I have been lugging them around ever since.

> Now, sobbing as I write, I look around for the chunk of my heart I had so ruthlessly tossed aside. I find it stuck in a corner tightly wound with knots of resentment. I understand fully that forgiving my Mother is the only way I can make any progress.
>
> Forgiving her allows me to peel back the first layer of pain. It's excruciatingly, but allowing myself to actual feel my feelings is a hell of a lot better than holding onto the pain.

"...and then the day came when the risk to remain tight in a bud was more painful than the risk it took to blossom."

- Anais Nin

The very next day I got myself to the home of mother's first cousin. Sitting across the kitchen table from her, I ask her how my grandparents treated my mother. She answered every question with brutal honesty. Learning the depth and breath of my mother's pain allowed me to release even more knots of resentment. As my heart opened, I was finally able to experience how much love I have for her.

That week I called my son in Texas. We talked about his job and he responded in his usual monotone voice. A little later he started talking about his new business venture in Austin's vibrant music scene. His voice became focused, animated and clear as a bell. This amount of enthusiasm was totally uncharacteristic of him. This must be a big deal.

Then he begins to tell me about a relationship he is pursuing with a woman he is interested in. I was stunned. These were major accomplishments for my first born. I was both proud and somewhat amazed.

When my son was quite young, he had a recurring nightmare, except that it happened during the day. (I have his permission to share this.) His day-mare took place in a barren landscape where a very tall woman held a large white sphere over her head. She felt to me like the White Witch of Narnia.

Below her, tiny ant-like people hide from her stone cold gaze by scurrying around, building houses made of sticks. His day-mare occurred often, causing him great anguish. We discussed it, drew it and analyzed it. Over the years, the only thing I understood clearly was that the sphere the woman held was locked up, frozen energy.

While listening to the enthusiasm in his voice, the image of the lady with the sphere came to mind. I realized, "He's no longer afraid of the Ice Queen. The sphere his lady was holding is beginning to melt, like the wicked witch at the end of the Wizard of Oz."

I heard a great deal of noise in the background and asked, "Are you driving while we are having this intense conversation?" He said he was. I suggested he pull over.

Then I hear, "Wow!" over the phone. I asked, "What?" He said, "You won't believe this. I pulled into a parking lot and directly in front of me is a statue of a woman holding a large ball over her head!"

Journaling about this later I thought "Isn't it amazing that my son would go through such profound changes immediately after I went through mine."

Then I wondered if one had anything to do with the other. Looking back in my journal I discover that my daughter left for college on September 6th. My son's birthday is... September 6th.

This was both terrifying and wonderful. Terrifying, because my son intuitively picked up on my many unresolved issues I had with my mother and created subconscious images that literally haunted him. Wonderful, because by working through my issues, I had unexpectantly helped to lighten his burden.

This helped me understand an aspect of Kabbalistic thought I had never fully grasped before. In the Kabbalah on the Tree of Life there are ten spheres of energy, similar to Chakras, known as Spheriot. One of the Spheriot is known as Hod, which means Reverberation.

Hod/Reverberation is explained as the resounding waves of energy that a thought or action sets into motion in the universe, similar to the ripples created from dropping a stone in a pool of water. Reverberation is the only explanation I can come up with on how my son picked up on the changes within me half a continent away.

Opening my heart and forgiving my mother created a profound shift. Unbeknownst to me, my son felt the shift. It lightened his load and helped him be more courageous. When we change, it reverberates out to those we love. I find this astounding.

This further informs my understanding of the only person we can change is ourselves. Once we actually change, you had better look out, because it sets other changes into motion. Once we stop wasting our time trying to change everybody else and focus our attention on actually changing ourselves, profound things can happen.

Be the change you wish to see in the world.
~ Gandhi

We *can* change the world just like Crosby, Stills, Nash and Young said, but only when we have the courage to make those changes within ourselves.

My new-found understanding of reverberation helps me comprehend the Butterfly Effect even more fully. Vaclav Havel, the imprisoned playwright who became the First President of the Czech Republic, once explained the Butterfly Effect to a World Economic Forum.

He described how the subtlety of an open mind and a willing spirit can create an effect that ripples out and changes our interrelationship with our world.

> *You have certainly heard of the Butterfly Effect. The notion that everything in the world is connected so mysteriously and comprehensibly, that the slightest movement of butterfly's wing in a single spot on this planet can unleash a typhoon thousands of miles away.*
>
> *We can not assume that our unique everyday actions have no consequence. We must believe, in all modesty, in the mysterious power of our own human being and its mysterious connection with the world's being.* [1]
>
> ~ *President Vaclav Havel*

My son felt my inner shift because of the love that connects us. Love is the glue. The *mysterious connection between our own and the world's being* is a profoundly different way of perceiving reality.

Our perception of the separation of mind and matter dates back Descartes in the 17th Century. His ideas, supported by Sir Isaac Newton became the foundation of classical physics.

The Descartes/Newton division of the universe, known as the Cartesian model, has dominated scientific thought, as well as our psyches for three hundred years.

Seeing ourselves as separate has brought us tremendous technological advances but, it has also delivered considerable damage to our planet.

The Cartesian model served as the basis of all scientific thought from the 17th into the 20th Century. But in dawning of the 20th Century new mind-blowing observations took place demonstrating the limitations of Descartes' theory. Physicists began to observe the atom.

Comprehending the inner workings of the atom presented a serious challenge to physicists' ability to understand the universe. Observing the atomic and subatomic world shook the minds of scientists to their very foundations.

Physicists became painfully aware that their basic concepts, language and their *whole way of thinking* were inadequate to describe atomic phenomena. Eminent physicists such as Albert Einstein, Niels Bohr and others where forced to comprehend space, time, matter and objects in entirely new ways.

Because of its complexities quantum physicists have had a difficult time explaining their observations of the atom to the general population. Dr. Fritof Capra is a quantum physicist who has worked tirelessly in this area, beginning with his book the *Tao of Physics* written in 1975.

> *The universe can no longer be seen as a machine, made up of individual, separate objects. As we penetrate into matter, nature does not show any isolated basic building blocks, but rather appears as a* ***web of relations*** *between the various parts of a unified whole.*
>
> *This unified whole can be divided into separate parts made of molecules*

> *and atoms. The molecules and atoms are made of particles. But here, at the level of particles, it becomes extremely difficult to separate any part of the universe from the whole.*
>
> *Subatomic particles are not 'things' but, the* ***interconnections*** *between 'things'. In quantum theory you do not end up with 'things'; you always deal with interconnections.*
>
> *Thus the modern physics conception of the* ***universe is as an interconnected web of relations.***
>
> *~ Fritof Capra*

I think most of us still perceive the universe from the 17th Century Cartesian perspective. Yet, mystics, saints and indigenous people of all cultures have intuitively perceived our interconnectness.

This we know:
all things are connected
like the blood which unites one family.

Whatever befalls the earth
befalls the sons of earth.

Man did not weave the web of life,
he is merely a strand on it.

Whatever he does to the web,
he does to himself. [3]

~ Chief Seattle

The new millennium has arrived and with it a call to stretch our minds around what our physicists learned from the atom over one hundred years ago.

We are here to awaken
from the illusion
of our separateness.
~ Thich Nhat Hanh

Could *awakening from the illusion of our separateness* be the new level of thinking Albert Einstein was referring to when he said ~

The significant problems that we face
can not be solved at the same level of thinking
with which they were created.
~ Albert Einstein

Could learning to see with new eyes and bigger hearts help us solve the significant problems we and our planet are facing?

~ 10 ~

The Orange Bird of Abundance

Life shrinks or expands in
direct proportion to one's courage.
~Anais Nin

I have been worrying about money lately. I woke up remembering two rather extreme dreams about my sense of abundance.

> I am attending a women's gathering in my friend's home. We are all standing in a small upstairs room dressed in gorgeous flowing gowns preparing for a relaxed extravaganza. The friend whose home we are in excuses herself to go down stairs. I follow a few steps behind her.
>
> Each room in the basement is filled to the brim with the beauty and bounty of life. There are gorgeous Renaissance paintings in the first room, tapestries covering every square inch in the next. In the third room there are happy bakers creating

> luscious pastries while magnificent displays of flowers are being arranged in the fourth. My friend is overseeing everything with such panache that I grow envious.
>
> In the second dream I am waiting to meet someone on a cold, grey November morning. I am surrounded by large wooden crates filled with apples. While waiting, I nonchalantly pick up an apple and take a bite.
>
> Instantly the owner screams, "What gives you the right to take one of my apples?" He is standing on top of a pile of wobbling crates with a funky adding machine in his arm. He is as nasty as can be and has lousy teeth.
>
> He goes on to say, "Now, you must go down the block and write a grant to make up for what you have taken from me. Write down this address."
>
> I am so angry my number dyscalculia kicks in. I can't write the numbers down in the right order for the life of me. The dream ends with him screaming at me even louder.

There are times when the clarity of dream imagery just knocks me out. The utter contrast of these two dreams reminds me of a Dickens novel. My subconscious has presented me with a perfect scenario of my struggle with abundance.

The basement is where many of us have placed the feminine. We have removed her from the upper floors of order and decorum and exiled her to the basement, much the same as Cinderella.

But why? Why would we do such a thing to such a lovely aspect of ourselves? Because through the eyes of Patriarchy - Eve, all women, Mary Magdalene, blacks, etc., have been labeled and blamed for all things sexual.

Yes, dealing with one's sexuality is huge, but scapegoating and blaming one's sexuality on *any* one else does not resolve or heal one's sexual dilemma. Blame merely keeps one's sexual energy stuck in Limbo.

Ramakrishna, the great Indian mystic once wrote, "If there were any two things in the world as difficult for human beings to deal with as sex, we'd never make it."

In Jewish Mysticism the feminine aspect of God is known as the Shekinah. The Shekinah is recognized as God's immanent presence. Webster's definition of immanent is: *1) living, remaining, or operating within; inherent 2) present throughout the universe: said of God: distinguished from Transcendent.*

Most of us, myself included, have separated the indwelling presence of God from most aspects of our lives because we are so terribly frightened of her/its/our power. Wouldn't it be wiser to approach the indwelling feminine presence with less fear and more love? Wouldn't listening be a better approach?

Back to the dream: My friend's basement is bursting at the seams with gifts from her feminine. But I am walking *behind* my friend, instead next to her, demonstrating I have yet to fully realize and accept the gifts my internal feminine has to offer.

After the plethora of textures, tastes and smells of the first dream, the next dream presents itself in stark contrast. There is a bone chilling mist permeating the scene. I encounter a stingy, nasty old man, who embodies every negative aspect of my grandfather. My grandfather is the one who became the male authority figure in my life after my Dad died.

I eat one lousy apple and he flips out. I obviously have a host of issues with this man. One day in real life, I unknowingly blocked the only access out of a parking lot. An angry, old man followed me for ten blocks, blaring his horn and yelling at me out his window. What can I say? I have issues.

After writing down the dreams, I went for a walk in the park. It was an absolutely gorgeous spring day. I arrived later than usual and the park was teaming with people. I began to worry whether I would be able to work through all the images in my head.

> I start walking. I am about half way around the lake when the old man with from my dream comes to mind. I have an intuitive flash and realize that the old man in the dream is not my grandfather. The miserable, nasty old man is me!
>
> I am the miserable one refusing to let go of my last shred. I have no idea what my last shred is but, whatever it is, I am holding onto it for dear life.
>
> I can feel the shred between the thumb and middle finger my right hand. The tension builds and begins to move from my fingers to my wrist and up my elbow. The tightness then moves quickly up my arm and into my right shoulder and it doesn't stop there. It moves toward the right side of my jaw. I can feel it now tightening my throat. I watch in horror, as my body spirals in toward lock down.
>
> Finally I think, "I wonder what would happen if I simply let go of the shred?' With that thought, the tension of my grip lessens. My hand unfurls like a flower, releasing the tension it held so

tightly with the rest of my body following.

In the midst of the release, a brilliant orange and yellow bird darts from behind and lands in a tree directly in front of me. The small outrageous orange bird then begins to chirp at me so loudly, it hardly seems possible for a bird that size. I am standing there in the middle of the park with my eyes glued on the bird and mouth open.

A couple walks by. The man looks at the bird and then at me saying, "The two of you are having quite a conversation. Whatever it is she is saying, you'd better be listening. Look, you're both wearing the same color."

Sure enough, the bird's breast and back are the exact same orange as the burnt orange shawl I have flung across my shoulder and down my back. Jung spoke of synchronicity, but this is off the hook.

How
did the rose
ever open its heart
and give to the world
all its beauty?

It felt the
encouragement of light
against its being,
otherwise
we all remain
too
frightened.

~ Hafiz

Could the universe get any louder or clearer? This miracle happened in broad day light with tons of other people around. What else is a miracle then the universe bending over backwards trying to get our attention? Alice Walker once wrote *in The Color Purple*:

> *God is inside you and inside everybody else. You come into the world with God, but only them that search for it inside, find it.*
>
> *Sometime it just manifest itself even if you are not looking... God ain't some thing you look at apart from anything else, including yourself.*
>
> *But one day it came to me: that feeling of being a part of everything, not separate at all. I knew that if I cut a tree, my arm would bleed.*
>
> *God is always making little surprises and springing them up on us when we least expect it...You ever notice that trees do everything to git our attention we do, except walk?*
>
> *I think it pisses God off if you walk by the color purple in a field somewhere and don't notice it.*
>
> *~Alice Walker*

In *The Matrix* Neo touches a mirror and liquid silver moves up his arm, shoulder, neck and side of his face. Just as the liquid is descending down his throat, they pull him out of it. That is what holding onto my last shred felt like it was doing to me.

What is this shred? What is it made of? And why am I clenching onto it so tightly? After giving it some thought I realize my shred is made from my resentment.

> There are moments when I can feel my body armor. I saw it in a dream once. It is thin and lightweight. I wear it like a sheath of mail chain over every muscle. It is woven out of past pains and fear of new ones. It is very good at its job. In fact, it is too good. It costs me plenty. I pay for it with my intimacy.

My grandfather was a nasty man. Yet, no matter how lousy he was, I need to let my resentment go. That is what the orange bird was saying to me, "Let that go. Let it go now! Holding onto that shit is killing you!"

Closing down, holding onto past pains and old grudges with our parents, sisters, friends, spouses, ex-spouses, grandparents, brothers and others are decisions we make. We create the prisons we get stuck inside of. We are the ones who pay the price of not forgiving others.

Our sadness and fear come from
being out of tune with love.
~ Hafiz

Who benefits the most when we forgive others? Most of the people we are pissed off at do not even know we are mad at them; either that or they died ages ago. Forgiving others does not free them, it frees us. Forgiveness dissolves our resentment and pain, allowing our hearts to open.

The Sufis often use the rose as a metaphor for the heart, opening our hearts allows to us to give and receive love from the core of our being. The depth of love and respect we have *for ourselves* has a profound effect on how we treat others. My gentle, younger son once wrote:

It is because I am a unique person
and I hold who I am so dear,

that I want to know more about
those around me.
~ N. Zev Minkoff

~

Just a few weeks after having this understanding, I fell back into my same ol' lousy patterns of lack and fear. Instead of opening my arms and embracing my orange bird of abundance, I freaked out and embraced my uncomfortable but, totally familiar stingy, old man.

> Both of my kids are home from college. We are working out of the change jar *all weekend* and it does not end on Monday or even on Tuesday. It does not end until I have to literally walk past my Grandfather's old the house to buy a dozen eggs.
>
> I lived one block away from where my grandfather used to live. His address was #273 and mine was #373. (How's that for karma?) Just as I am about to walk past his house I stop. Standing there I take a deep breath and decide to declare a truce. Saying a prayer, I bend down to touch the earth with my right hand. I let my anger and resentment flow from my hand into the earth.
>
> Looking up I notice a patch of Lily of the Valley growing under the bushes in his front yard. I walk over, pick a flower and stick it behind my ear. I smell its sweet fragrance all day long.

I now know the fragrance of peace. Peace smells like Lily of the Valley. The path leading toward my stingy, nasty old man is now closed. I am making different choices; choices based on faith and trust in my new friend, my small, outrageous Orange Bird of Abundance.

~ 11 ~

Instant Karma

Instant Karma's gonna get you.
Gonna knock you off your feet.
Better recognize your brother
Everyone you meet. [1]

~ *John Lennon*

Our choices open and close the petals of our hearts like the aperture of a camera. We are constantly making minor adjustments as we decide how much of light, love and life-force we wish to allow into our lives.

> *Our unhappiness is the consequence of our actions. Our actions are the consequence of our choice. Our choices are what take us further away or closer to the Source of Life within us.* [2]
>
> ~ *Jean-Yves Leloup*

Soul building is being mindful of our choices while taking responsibility for their consequences as they unfold before our eyes.

The soul exists and is built entirely
out of attentiveness.
~ Mary Oliver

If we wish to know whether a decision we made was a good one or bad one, we need only to observe the effect it creates. If our decision creates a negative effect, another opportunity will invariably present itself.

Then we have to ask ourselves, "Do I make the same choice and fall into the same hole or do I choose to make a different choice this time?" Our choices create our Karma. John Lennon sang very clearly about the universe giving us immediate feed back on whether we are on the right track or not.

Instant Karma's gonna get you.
Gonna look you right in the face.
You better get yourself together.
Join the human race.
~ John Lennon

Once we're paying attention, we begin to notice how capable the universe is at helping us make more informed decisions. Why then do I so often look to others to see what is right for me if I am able to receive information directly from the universe itself?

If I am paying 100% attention to being on my thread, I can not be paying attention to what anyone else should be doing. No matter how tempting it is or how noble my intentions are, I do not have the right to tell anyone else what to do.

Making our own decisions can be

terrifying. Free will is the greatest burden God has given us. It is also our greatest gift. Free will is the power of our choices. Our choices create our world. Free will is *the force* Joseph Campbell wrote about and George Lucas made famous. Each of us needs learn how to wield our own light saber.

Take the last ten days of my life for example. Eleven days ago I was enthusiastically editing a few chapters from this book for my acupuncturist to read. I felt my energy grow stronger and clearer as I typed. I was getting very excited thinking about my book going out into the world.

We Can Change the World by Crosby, Stills, Nash and Young was playing loudly in my head. I saw and felt my internal flame igniting small bonfires in others. The fire within grew into a brilliant powerful blaze..........and then, I got scared and snuffed out the fire.

I put a lid on my flame. I unconsciously closed down my very own power station by sucking out my life-force. I did not know I did it at the time, but I did it, nevertheless. Now observe, if you will, what the universe did to me over the course of the following ten days to get my ass back on track.

Instant Karma's gonna get you
Gonna knock you right on the head.
You better get yourself together
Pretty soon, you're gonna be dead.

~John Lennon

Sun I want to go to a movie, but discover I have a flat tire.

Mon AAA comes and changes my flat. Meanwhile, my computer (with my entire book on it) won't even boot up. I unplug it and take it to a nearby computer repair shop. After dropping it off, I have a fender bender in the parking lot with a nice guy. I apologize. We exchange phone numbers and go to buy a new tire. I need to buy two new tires.

Tues I call a friend and tell her I am having a hard time. We go to hear Matthew Fox discuss overcoming passive aggression by tapping into one's moral outrage. It is exactly what I need to hear. My energy shifts.

Wed My BOSE Surround Sound System at work breaks down, as does my washing machine. My son and his new girlfriend arrive from Texas for a family wedding.

Thurs I drive my son, his new girlfriend and my younger son to Niagara Falls. On the way home, I have another fender bender. This time it's with a young woman in her brand new Toyota Corolla. My stomach starts to feel lousy.

Fri All is calm, although my stomach still isn't right.

Sat My daughter-in-law asks about my book. I talk for an hour, non-stop while she listens patiently. Later, at the rehearsal dinner with my plate brimming with delicious food, my stomach lets me know, "No way, Jose."

Sun I am up early, facing my demons and writing like

mad. My digestive tract is in terrible shape. I finally tune into what's up. I understand my problem. *I am scared.* I am a powerful being and my power scares the shit out of me, literally and figuratively.

I am scared because, I have a sacred task to fulfill. I may be frightened and I may be in awe, but no matter how frightened I may be, I may no longer hide my light or my truth. My job is to let my light shine, as brightly as possible, no matter what.

I am going to see Al Gore give a speech the next day. I decide to speak my truth by writing him a letter about healing the planet by taking responsibility for our choices gives us *the courage to change the things we can.* The more I write, the less frightened I become. The less frightened I become, the better I and my stomach feels.

I attend the gracious wedding of my creative, blended family. Love makes us all so beautiful. The icing on the cake came when two dear old friends made a surprise visit. What a delight. Before going to sleep, I edit my letter to Al.

Mon I wake up remembering one of the most intense dreams I have ever had. I pick up my friend and share the dream with her as we drive a few hours to see Al Gore. Here is a man who is fulfilling his life's work.

Tues I have an appointment with my dermatologist who also happens to have a Masters Degree in Creativity. He asks me what's up. I tell him I have been working on a book. He lights up, telling me I should check out self publishing @ *iuniverse.com*. I laugh out loud knowing I have just made it through my crisis.

What helped me change my reality? How important was the love of family and friends? How did my daughter-in-law's patient listening help me move through so much of my stuff?

And how in the world was I in the company of Matthew Fox, all my children, current friends, dear old friends, Al Gore and my creative dermatologist all in the course of ten days? Sure, there was a family wedding, but still.

The way I see it, the universe bent over backwards sending me all the love and support I needed. What is odd is, I could have missed it. If I had not been so out of whack, I could have taken for granted the tremendous love and support my family, friends and mentors gave me.

Thankfully, I did not. My intention is to remain mindful and grateful for all the love I receive and give every day.

All you need is love.

~ *The Beatles*

~ 12 ~

The Red Earth Dream

The evening following my family wedding, I had one of the most intense dreams of my life. But, I did not have time to write it down. So I shared it with my friend as we drove to see Al Gore.

> The dream begins with me registering at a place of personal growth and transformation called the Omega Institute. While standing in line, an old flame walks up, looking more handsome than ever and asks me to dance. I ask myself, "Am I still married?"
>
> Inside my head I hear a resounding "No!" I dance with the man. Off to the side I see and hear my ex husband flipping out. He rants and raves as he walks past me with a woman and up a flight of stairs. A few minutes later the woman walks down saying, "To hell with that." and walks away.
>
> A small old woman appears telling me to follow her. We walk next to a large building made of thick grey stones. I turn and face a stone wall. To my right is a black iron cross stuck in the ground. The old woman tells me to pull up on the cross. As I do, one of the large grey stones slides forward creating a chute.
>
> I slide down the stone and land on reddish

brown earth. In the center is a large oval pool. There is a number of people standing in and around the pool. Everyone is relaxed and enjoying themselves. Soon the others leave. I am standing alone by the pool.

I sense a presence in the space and realize I am about to be tested. Standing on the edge of the pool, I am told to step in. I step into the pool and the water turns solid under my feet. This freaks me out, so I turn the earth back into water and climb out.

I am told to step in again. I do. The water again turns into reddish brown earth. I enjoy how cool and solid it feels under my feet and walk away from the church on solid red earth.

I am now walking in a field with a male friend. Soon I sense people are chasing us. We begin to run. We get as far as a thick wooden door through which we can escape. My friend hands me a black iron lock, letting me know it is my job to attach the lock to the door.

I try to attach the iron lock to the door with a short, Philips head screw. I am so frightened I drop the screw. I take a deep breath, find the screw and focus even more intently. I am holding the lock onto the door with my left hand, while focusing on the head of the screw and turning it with my right. It takes every ounce of concentration I have to attach the lock.

Focusing my full attention on the head of the screw calmed me down significantly. I notice am no longer afraid. Instead of running out the door and locking it behind me, I turn to see who has been chasing me.

The dream shifts. It is winter. I am standing on the side of a road with winding S-curves. Three guys are spraying gasoline on the road, making the road slick and slippery. Two guys get into a car, drive it as fast as they can and then hit the brakes. These jerks are doing donuts on the S-curves and they're having the time of their lives!

> I am watching all this from the side of the road when a man with white hair dressed in red, white and blue goes riding by on a ski-do. He then falls off the ski-do and lands face first in a pile of snow at my feet.

The dream begins with me walking into a place that represents change and transformation. I am immediately challenged to revisit a difficult decision I made fifteen years ago. I cared a great deal about the man who asked me to dance.

Not pursuing this relationship was the right decision. Because of my guilt, I gave away too much of my personal power into my husband's hands. I now realize giving him so much power was the beginning of my demise. But that was then, and this is now. In the dream, I realize I am free to be with whomever I choose.

I am then led by a small old woman to the ground floor of what I consider to be a church. The old woman reminds me of the tough ol' crone who taught me Jungian psychology. Pulling up on the iron cross opens the way into my inner my castle/church. I drop onto the ground floor surrounding an oval pool, symbolizing the feminine.

The people there are relaxed and elegant. The moment they leave I sense a presence and wonder, "Am I alone with God?" I am told to step into the pool. I think, "This is like stepping off the ledge. It is a test of faith, but not about my faith in God. Now I am being tested in how much faith I have in myself."

My stepping into the pool causes the water

to turn into earth. I think it is supposed to be water; so I change it back. I am told to step in again. It turns solid beneath my feet. I leave it alone. Does this mean I can now have the power to create my own solid ground beneath my feet? Cool.

The man I am walking with hands me an iron lock, imparting to me that this is my job to do. He is Jungian terms, my animus, a positive, inner male figure.

I am a recovering Catholic and two long black iron crosses could certainly be seen as phallic symbols. Being more Jungian than Freudian, I see the iron crosses more as swords, the sword being a masculine symbol of discernment. Putting the lock into my hands, my inner male lets me know I am fully capable of handling this.

Having to focus my full attention on the head of the screw calmed me down to the point where I was able to see how my fears were distorting the situation. I no longer needed to lock the gate to have control. Being calm and centered allowed me to be in more control of myself and my boundaries.

Not indulging my fears, as it turns out, is what helped me become clear and courageous enough to turn and face who was approaching.

Let me assert my firm belief that the only thing we have to fear is fear itself.
~Franklin D. Roosevelt

Then the question is, who was chasing me? Or to look at it from a different point of view, who is it I am running away from? Eventually I realize who I am so afraid of, but not until I learn some pretty tough but valuable lessons.

Indulging my fears led me to believe I was being chased. So, does giving into fear create more fear? Is fear also in the eye of the beholder? I had no idea the extent to which my fears shaped my reality.

Proust has pointed out that the predisposition to love creates its own objects. Is not the same also true of fear?
~ Elizabeth Bowen

There is a Sesame Street book entitled *There's Monster at the End of This Book*. In it Grover warns the reader about a terrible monster at the end of the book, imploring us not to turn the page. Of course we have to turn the page.

He then pleads for us to, "Stop Turning the Pages." but alas, what can we do? We get to the end of the book and what do we discover? Why Loveable furry ol' Grover is the monster at the end of the book.

I had to accept that giving into my fears created the monsters I was so afraid of. As I turn to look at the three people approaching, I wonder who they may be. All I know is - they make me very uncomfortable. But I am no longer afraid of them. Maybe that is who they are. They are the parts of myself I am not comfortable with!

If the only person I have any control of is myself, how do I deal with those aspects of myself even I am afraid of? These are aspects of myself I have put away because others have let me know they can be too much. But, where do I hide me?

We have met the enemy
and he is us. [1]
~ Pogo

So instead of rejecting my uncomfortable aspects, I decide to approach them with compassion. If I can *be there* for my kids when they are in pain, can I not also be there for myself when I am hurting? Can I pick up where my parents left off?

I can choose to stay pissed off at my mother for not *being there* for me when I had an earache at age seven. Or I can forgive her and learn to be there for myself no matter what. My mother has been dead for close to forty years. If I don't respond to my pain with love and compassion, I am not so sure I will allow anyone else to either.

Forgiveness multiples and melts rigid postures.
Try again and again with self-forgiveness.

Be the kind parent to yourself
you may not have had. [2]
~ SARK

I am officially unsubscribing to the *Tough Shit* method of existence. It is an utter waste of time. I and many of us walk around pretending we are not wounded, hoping our pain will simply go away if we ignore it long enough. So tell me, "How's that working for ya?"

Wasn't having our needs ignored what

initially caused our pain? Ignoring my needs feeds my anger, addiction, blame and self-pity. Ignoring my needs is what perpetrates my inherited cycles of neglect.

I am learning to respond to my needs with love and compassion, even though my parents were not able to 24/7. Can anyone protect me from experiencing pain 24/7? Do I even want to be protected from experiencing pain? Isn't pain and separation what motivates me to seek God?

Maybe this is what Marion Woodman meant when she said, "God comes in through the wound." Can I love myself even when I am in pain? Can I trust in love enough to let go of my fear?

We can only learn to love
by loving.
~ Iris Murdoch

~13~

Meetings with Remarkable Men[1]

At some point
your relationship with God

will become like this:
Next time you meet

Him in the forest
or on a crowded street

there won't be anymore
"Leaving."

That is, God will climb into
your pocket.

You will simply just take
YourSelf
Along![2]
~Hafiz

I had a discussion in mid-December with a friend who was a published author. She explained to me the difference between traditional and self publishing. While listening to her I grew increasingly agitated learning I could lose control of my book if I went with traditional publisher. That night I had the following dream.

> I am standing outside a store slipping purple beads onto a nylon thread. I enjoy watching the beads as they slide, interlock and fall into a perfect double spiral in my hand. My ex, who is standing nearby, gives me a hard time for not noticing how short my thread has become. I go into the store to buy more thread.
>
> Once inside, I notice different strands of beads hanging on nails in the wall. One has green with purple plastic Mardi Gras beads. Next to it is a necklace made of small carved animals with black beads in between. The sales lady (who reminds me of my mother) approaches. She is trying to sell me the animal necklace. I tell her, "No, thank you."
>
> She ignores me and folds the animal necklace inside an old blanket. She then places the blanket inside a beat up leather suitcase. She tells me to, "Return the suitcase in a week." I hit the roof saying, "I am not interested in that beat up leather suitcase. I don't want it or anything in it!"

This dream addresses my anxiety about losing control over my book pretty directly. Yet, it also addresses an even more intrinsic issue.

If I am totally enthralled with the form the double strand of purple beads is making as they spiral in my hand, why do I even listen to what anyone else has to say? Why am I willing to leave this beauty to go into the shop?

Do I not deem myself worthy of holding a strand of the universe in my hand? Can I not appreciate the loveliness I am holding without giving in to the anxiety that I must go somewhere else to find what I need?

You have within you an Egypt, miles of riverside canebed, the source of all sweetness.

Yet, you worry whether candy will come from a store outside yourself. [3]

~ *Rumi*

We come into this world with the universe in the palm of our hand. Somewhere along the way, we drop the ball or let someone talk us out of it. Who was it that came up with the concept of original sin? And why do we listen?

Once we stop paying attention to our thread, we lose touch with our souls and forget our way back to the source of our magnificence. Finding our thread helps us remember who we are and what we came here to do. Our thread keeps us connected to our true nature, as well as to God.

A few weeks after having this dream, I had the following experience:

> It is late in the afternoon of Christmas Eve. After running around shopping all day, I make one more stop. I run into my local dollar store for a quart of oil for my car. While pouring it into my crank case I notice it is coming out thin and red. This isn't oil. It's transmission fluid!
>
> I speak to a man in the parking lot. He tells me I should be OK driving my car the half block to

my house but, then *to not drive it anywhere.* No problem. It is 4:30 pm on Christmas Eve. The doors of commercial USA have just slammed shut.

I rest then make a delicious turkey dinner with my kids. They set the table with a nice tablecloth, the good china and fancy napkins. While eating, the temporary crown on my front tooth comes loose. I take it off and place it on the table. Together we watch *It's a Wonderful Life.*

While cleaning up, I take the tablecloth off. Now, do I shake it out over the garbage like I usually do? Oh hell no! I shake it out over the toilet and then flush it. That's right; I flushed the temporary crown for my front tooth down the toilet.

The next morning is Christmas Day. I don't have a car to drive to my sister's house or a front tooth. There couldn't be a better time for my inner critic to kick into overdrive but, maybe because it was Christmas Eve, I had the presence of mind to work with my inner critic instead.

I sit down with my journal. I understand I need to write poetry instead of my usual prose to capture the nuanced streams of thought flowing within me. It reminds me of when I used to French braid my daughter's hair.

Being here empty and open
is where I need to be.

No one is talking down to me.
I am OK being just the way I am.

No more either/or.
I am a hero *and* an asshole
and I'm still evolving.

Closing my heart when I make a mistake
doesn't change anything.

Criticism only wraps the chains
of fear tighter.

I need to love and be loved
as I am.

Writing strikes a chord, bringing to mind my three deepest dreams. In the first I am standing outside a shop with purple beads in my hand. In the second I am standing at my Beloved's side, refusing to leave him to go teach reading to kids. In the third I am standing in the entrance of a gate. I then turn to face the three people who are approaching.

Hey, it's the three guys from my dream. The guys who were spraying gasoline, doing donuts and driving the ski-doo!

It then dawns on me that these three guys have an awful lot to do with me.

> *It is only when we have the courage to face things exactly as they are, without any sort of self-deception or illusion, that a light will develop out of events, by which the path to success may be recognized.* 4
>
> *~ The I Ching*

It is Christmas morning. I borrow a friend's car and drive to my sister's house. I only had to endure one rendition of *All I want for Christmas is my two front teeth* from my brother-in-law. We had a lovely time. The next day I drive my car to a service station run by some guys a close friend tells me I can trust. They drain the transmission fluid and steam clean the engine.

The car starts that day but, not the next. They suggest a new battery. I buy one. The car starts fine on day two but, not on day three. “Houston, we have a problem.” It is December in Buffalo and to mention that it is cold seems redundant. I have not been to work in days and I am getting nowhere fast.

Meantime, I am still trying to figure out who or what the three guys from my dream represent. Finally I remember a Jungian technique called Active Imagination that could help.

It works by writing a question to one’s dream figure, pulling one’s ego back and writing down what one’s subconscious has to say. It comes in handy when needing to coax more information out of dream figures.

Me to My Guys~ So, are you guys having fun?

Guys~ Yeah, It’s fun. We’re just blowing off some steam.

Me~ What you’re doing is really dangerous. Aren’t you afraid of getting hurt?

Guys~ Nay, we don’t really give a shit.

Me~ Are you drunk?

Guys~ Sure we’re drunk.

Me~ Why?

Guys~ Why not?

Me~ Isn’t there someone or something you care

about?

Guys~ Some, but not enough.

Me~ What do you care about?

Guys~ Drinking.

Me~ What about women? There must be some women you care about and who care about you.

Guys~ There is someone.

Me~ Yes. Who?

Guys~ You.

Me~ Me?

Guys~ Yeah, we wouldn't mind if you cared about us again.

Me~ Again?

Guys~ Yeah, you used to care about us. You used to be with us here in Tonawanda. Then you went away and got too snooty for us. We're not too sure who it is you are trying to be, but we know who you really are. You are a girl from Tonawanda and you need to be OK with that.

Me ~ You're right. I have been a snot.

Guys ~ You know the saying, "No matter where you go, there you are."

Me~ Yeah, I'm afraid so.

Guys~ Are we really so bad? Or are you just not used to being with regular guys like us?

Me~ You guys are pretty reckless.

Guys~ We are. It's just that no one has paid any attention to us in a really long time. We get pretty crazy hanging around with just each other.

We pretend we don't care but actually, we care a lot. So, don't give up on us, OK? We get self-destructive when it feels like you've given up on us. We just need to know you care.

My Brothers

Me~ Ok, may I talk to my little brother?

Me to Brother M~I want to start by saying how sorry I am for the lousy way I treated you growing up. I was mean and cruel and I am very sorry.

Can you forgive me? Can we work on our relationship? I am going to start behaving more like your big sister. But, after all the terrible things I've done to you, I'm afraid you may reject me.

Brother M~ Marcia, when you reach through your fears to me, you reach through my fears as well. I need my big sister. I need your loving touch.

Me to Brother M~ I am grateful to hear that. I am here for you.

My heart opens as I reach out to him. The more love I give him, the more love I receive.

Me to my 1st cousin G~ I enjoy being in touch with you again.

Cousin G~ I appreciate your love and attention. Our relationship means a lot to me. Please know I love you and your sister as much as I love my own sisters.

I then write to my big brother. We were very close growing up. Then he went to Vietnam. He said he did not have a bad tour of duty. Yet, after returning home and about to take on a full time job, he had a mental break down. He has not been mentally stable since.

Me to Brother K~ I love you. Tell me, was that you dressed like Uncle Sam in my dream?

Brother K~ How did you know? Uncle Sam did a real number on me, Marcia. That's why I'm face first in the snow.

Me~ It's about time I understood the truth. Forgive me for being so stubborn and so blind.

Brother K~ We have always been close. Just remember, under the snow is the heart of one, who loves you so.

Me- I am finally here. What can I do?

Brothers K & M - We both need your love. We both need you to be more understanding and accepting of us as we are. You have no idea how hard it is to be a man. You never got to see Dad as just a regular guy because, we where all so very young when he died.

So, here we are, your brothers.
Just love us as we are.
Here we are, your brothers.
We love you as you are.

I honestly did not understand the full extent to which Vietnam triggered my older brother's mental anguish. I had misunderstood and thought taking on the full time job is what tripped him out. I am extremely sorry about how wrong I have been.

The very next morning I am hanging around the service station as they work on my car, when in walks a tall man with white hair who reminds me of my favorite uncle. We are introduced. His name is...*Uncle* Bill. He works for the Mayor's Impact Team. I ask him what the Impact Team does.

Uncle Bill, who is at least sixty-five years old replies, "We go around closing down crack houses. We also work a lot with squatters and homeless people. Most of the guys are Vets from Vietnam and Desert Storm. They're really good guys. They just don't want to be part of the system anymore."

For emphasis he says again, "They're really good guys who just don't want to be part of the system." We talk a little more. As our conversation draws to a close I reach out to shake his hand and thank him for the work he does. He then bows, kisses my hand and walks out the door.

Some pretty fat tears start rolling down my cheeks. They are tears of sadness for my brother and the countless Vets who suffer every single day of their lives. They are tears of shame for all the years I misunderstood my brother's anguish and pain.

They are also tears of gratitude for Uncle Bill and other human beings like him who dedicate their lives to being of service. There are also tears of thankfulness for Carl Jung and his insightful methods capable of unlocking the treasures one's subconscious holds.

I am grateful to my older brother for showing me my father needed to be loved, as well as give it. I had placed my father so high on a pedestal I could not see him or his needs. No wonder I have struggled so with the men in my life.

When I finally met *my inner guys* and saw how much pain my arrogance had created within and without, I felt like Scrooge in the *Christmas Carol*, grateful to have a second chance.

I have always accused my grandfather of being the bastard in the family. Until today I have never owned up to the part I played in all of this.

The guys at the service station eventually discovered the culprit. It was one very soggy alternator, dripping with transmission fluid.

The time spent between Christmas and New Years that winter cost me over a thousand dollars in missed work and repairs. A thousand dollars compared to the value of reestablishing a more loving relationship with my brothers, cousin, uncle and father............Priceless.

Nor do I underestimate the value of finding good, honest men who are now not only my mechanics, but also my friends.

Perhaps all of the dragons of our lives are princesses who are only waiting to see us once beautiful and brave?

Perhaps everything terrible is in its deepest being, something that needs our love.
~ Rainer Maria Rilke

My Knight

Months passed and a small problem at work has mushroomed into a big one. I have been a consultant for an agency for a number of years and am in the process of being hired as an employee. This requires a more thorough background check.

Having worked for the City and other agencies in the past I assumed there would be no problem, but this is a State job. A misdemeanor from 1969 has come into question. I may not return to work until it is straightened out.

For some reason I have to prove that my misdemeanor was in fact, a misdemeanor. The infraction took place over 35 years ago and all the records have since been destroyed. I have to go downtown to a City Court Judge to straighten everything out.

It is now the second week without working. I am waiting around and trying real hard not to let this situation get the best of me. Sitting down I write in my journal, asking my inner masculine for some help.

> While writing, I can see in my mind's eye a knight lying on the ground on his back. He rises to standing. He is holding a sword in his right hand. He then places his hands on each side of the hilt of the sword and presses the sword firmly into the earth. He looks me right in the eye saying:

> **Knight**~ No more! No More Now. You need to get back to your original job of writing your book. Enough! You need to be doing your real work.
>
> I am here to help you be grounded and strike a balance. You can be firm without being afraid. You did everything you needed to do.
>
> **Me**~ It is an honor to meet you. I appreciate your being here. Your focus and dedication remind me of Russell Crowe in *The Gladiator*.
>
> **Knight**~ Yes, but I am different. I am not in some movie. I am here within you. I am here to give you strength and courage. I am here to demonstrate how to dig deep and be grounded. I will find helpers for you, but remember, they are extensions of me. Do not confuse them for me. I am the one you who is here for you. I am always at your side.

At that moment the phone rings. It is work. The lawyer for the State is looking over my information and needs a few more papers on his desk by 4:00 pm this afternoon! This means I need to get downtown and then out to the suburbs. It is already 1:30 pm and my car is at my mechanics.

I try to ride my bike to the repair shop, but discover the bike is not pedaling right. I make this discovery while riding pass my old house where my ex is backing out of his driveway. I ask him for a ride. He graciously drives me to the bank and then to the service station. Thanking him, I hop out.

My car is not ready yet. My anxiety must have been palpable. The owner, who I have mentioned earlier, must have sensed my distress. He asks one of the guys in the shop to drive me downtown, telling him to wait for me until I get what I need. Now, these guys are great, but they are willing to drive me downtown *and wait for me*!?! I am very grateful.

I am driven downtown. I gather all the necessary papers and am driven back to the shop where my car is ready and waiting for me. It is 3:45. I go flying down the expressway.

As I get closer to work I notice a flock of large birds out my window and wonder, “Hawks at a time like this?” I park and rush toward the front door. The flock of birds flies overhead. I look up. It is not a flock of hawks. It is a flock of vultures. What a metaphor. I hand the papers in precisely at 4:00 pm.

Not until the next morning, as I sit down and write, do I acknowledge and appreciate what had transpired on my behalf the day before.

Me ~You really came through for me.

Knight~ I said I would.

Me~ Yes, but you came through immediately!

Knight~ You needed someone to stand up and defend you.

Me~ But all those men showed up as well.

Knight~ We all appreciate the opportunity to truly be of service. It lets us be our best selves.

Me~ You are a man of your word. I thank you.

Knight~ It is an honor and a pleasure.

This was all very dramatic and I am very grateful, but it did make me wonder why I needed such a clear demonstration of how to stand up for myself?

After some contemplation, I became aware of the crux of my issue. My sweet, kind, loving father never stood up to my mother. He never stood his ground or asked for what he wanted and needed. If my father had had the courage to stand up to my mother, my family's dynamics would be dramatically different, but he never did. This does not mean I never can.

I now have my very own inner knight demonstrating how to place my sword in the ground and say, "Enough. Enough Now. No More." Hopefully, I am passing this understanding onto my children.

But something must have changed. People are treating me differently. It must be my body language. Until I had this experience, I like most women, never even knew I had a sword, let alone how to use one.

The more we as women are able to reclaim our inner strength and create firmer boundaries, the sooner we will be able to create a more balanced world inside and out.

Inner Dave

The other night I dreamt I was in a group hug at a Dave Matthews concert.

I ask one of the guys if Dave is married. (He is

in real life.) He responds, "Dave isn't seeing anyone right now. It's hard for him to tell if someone loves him for who he is or for who *they* want to be."

Once I was fully awake I understood Dave's concern. Do I love smart, creative, powerful men for themselves or do I love them to gain access to my own inner masculine?

Inner Masculine~ Love is a two way street, my dear. This is not just about you getting your needs met. That's not love. That's selfishness. Love is the tenderness you feel for your brothers.

You don't love me so that one day I'll be your knight. No. No. No. Love loves for its own sake. Love takes risks. There are no guarantees.

I am learning to accept my inner masculine as he is, not as a super star, nor as a dejected child, but as a regular man.

Inner Dave~ Do you love me for me or for yourself? If you love me for yourself, then admit it. Don't waste your time giving me your energy and hoping I'll give it back to you.

Love your Self. Stop giving me and other men all your love, power and admiration. Go ahead. Be all that you are. Don't just admire it in me. Be it! Become it! Own it! **Be true to your Self!**

Stop asking me and other men to carry your projections for you. Take the risk. No one else can do it for you. I am doing the best I can, but I am just one guy. I am asking you and your women friends to step it up! Go ahead, please. **Speak Up! Fall in love with your Self. Carpe Diem- Seize the Day.**

Take the risk of being my own conscious, talented self!?! Sing the truth? Do live music at my book promotions? Hell, yes!!! Gathering my wits about me, I open Hafiz and read:

Perhaps for just one minute of the day,
it maybe of value to torture yourself

with thoughts like "I should be doing a
hell of a lot more with my life than I am,

cause I'm so damn talented. "But remember,
just for one minute out of every day. 5
~ *Hafiz*

I am happy to report I bought my little brother a birthday present. It was a statue of a young boy for his garden with the word Gentleness across the back. I did not pack it very carefully and it arrived in a thousand pieces yet, he told me he appreciated the thought. We are making progress. I am reaching out and he is letting me in.

The morning I mailed him the statue I went to a school to teach. I set up six African drums outside for the class to play. We ended up playing with a parachute instead.

We lifted the parachute up over our heads, let it billow and then tucked it under our bottoms as we sat down, creating a magical world of children investigating clovers, dandelions, ants and each other. We enjoyed each moment, one after the other.

My Man

I had a dream about a remarkable man the other night.

I am working on a project with a nice looking man with dark hair. His eyes sparkle like sunlight on river stones. Our energies work so nicely together I soon realize something quite delightful is happening.

Suddenly, a billboard zooms into view with huge hands opening and closing and flashing bright lights that read, **"Don't Be Too Grabby."** It is so ugly and blaring we both run away.

While writing this in my journal I hear a voice from within saying, "You don't need to grab. Don't try so hard to keep it. Let it be. Let it move. "

The one you are looking for
is already here.

You don't need to grab
what you already have.

You don't need to take
what is already yours.

You need to receive
with gratitude
what
life is
offering you."

To look at a person without attachment allows us to see that person as the gift they truly are. Nothing is owed to us. Everything is given... Thinking we can possess a person or object is an illusion. True relationship is being in a harmonious, conscious, loving relationship with what is. 6

~ Jean-Yves Leloup

The following Monday at 9 o'clock in the

morning I am leading a Team Building workshop. Three people walk into the room, take an instrument and start playing. Within five minutes we are jamming like mad. By 9:20 I am already singing a chant to Yemanja, the Yorba Goddess of the oceans. There are only seven of us in the room. I get that this is one talented, cohesive group and that we are going to rock.

After two more rhythms, I am up and dancing with everyone. Usually, I need to keep the beat going for everyone to dance to but, this nice looking man with dark hair and eyes is holding down the rhythms so solidly on my drum I am free to dance. Needless to say, I am delighted.

Our time together comes to an end far too quickly. Still excited, everyone helps carry the drums and instruments to my car. While walking we talk about going out to jam sometime. The man who drummed so well mentions he can not go because, he has just moved here from California and has new young kids. Then it hits me. He is the guy from my dream.

Meeting you was like diving into
a deep, clear pool.

I should have recognized you from the dream
but, I got all confused seeing you in a real man.

We played so well together.
Making Music! Dancing!

We had a lotta fun.
Time's up.

Gotta run.

Wait! Wait!
We've just begun.

You mention having
new young kids.

Firm boundaries help me
not get
as strung out.

But, here is where
I get stuck.

Here between
loving
&
letting go.

What do I do now?
I can't reach out
or follow.

Clinging feels shitty.
So does chasing after.

What do I do now?
Where do I go?

Why not met me in here
where we first met.
Meet me in here where it's
brilliant and wet.

Like your eyes?
It's good to see you.

It's good to be seen.
I am glad you found me.

Now what?

Now comes the hard part. Are you going to keep looking for me on the outside?

Like a million times before? No, not any more.

Then, what are you going to do?

I am going to ask myself where can I always find you?

I let go
and
find

you
are
already
here

waiting
for

me.

~

Love's gift can not be given,
it waits to be received.
~ Rabindranath Tagore

~

Lovers don't finally meet somewhere.
They are in each other all along.
~ Rumi

There is some kiss we want,
with our whole lives.
~ Rumi

~

I am not I.
I am this one
walking beside me whom I do not see,
whom at times I manage to visit,
and whom at other times I forget;
the one who remains silent when I talk,
the one who forgives, sweet, when I hate,
the one who takes a walk when I am indoors,
the one who will remain standing when I die.
~ Juan Ramon Jimenez

~ 14 ~

We Are the Ones We've Have Been Waiting For [1]

~June Jordan

Here we are, following our fates... until we
hear a drum begin, grace entering our lives.

We feel the call of God... They say, "You may
feel happy enough where you are

but please, we can't do without you any
longer"! So we walk along inside the rose

being pulled the way lakes and rivers are.

My guide, my soul, your only sadness is when
I am not walking with you. In deep silence,

with some exertion to stay in your company,
I could save you a lot of trouble. [2]

~ Rumi

This book was on the verge of going to print, when my daughter came home with a copy of Hermann Hesse's *Demain*. After re-reading it I realized, I need to revisit an important issue.

I need to revisit fulfilling one's sacred task. What I need to say is- we, both you and I, can no longer hide from our light or our truth. Coming to terms with just how powerful each and every one of us is, *is an idea whose time has come.*

Our deepest fear is
not that we are inadequate.

Our deepest fear is that
we are Powerful Beyond Measure.

It is our light, not our darkness
that most frightens us...

We were born to make manifest
the glory of God that is within us.

It is not just in some of us;
it is in everyone.

And as we let our own light shine,
we unconsciously give other people
permission to do the same.

As we are liberated from our own fears,
our presence automatically liberates others. [3]

~ Marianne Williamson

This is what we discover when we follow our path to the Source of Life within us. Reconnecting to our Source allows us to understand and accept that *we were born to make manifest the glory of God that is within us.*

Every single one of us came here to shine our light and be true to the unique aspect of God that dwells within us. Bringing forth our light and our truth is our sacred task.

This is no easier for me to say then it is for you to hear. I am the one who keeps running away from shining my light and truth, remember?

Every time I do run away, the universe comes in, finds where I am hiding and drags me back out into the light of day. The universe is doing this continually to each and every one of us, making sure we manifest our full glory.

The more we practice being true to all that we are, the more we remember our life's purpose. Each of us is the *only one* who can remember our life's purpose, which is why following our own path is of such vital importance. Walking our path leads us to our treasure.

The ego's real job is to serve the true Self. When one's ego is thick and unmovable, we tend to believe this is who we are. Yet, working on oneself allows our ego to become thinner and more pliable. There are moments when one's ego can be so thin it is transparent; allowing the full glory of one's being to shine through.

From a Kabbalistic point of view, working on oneself involves peeling back the husks of darkness, known as klippot, that cover and hide our light. Peeling back the husks of misunderstanding allows us to reveal and remember our divine spark.

Each of us is being called. Each of us is being asked to bring forth our truest sense of Self to be of service to each other and our world. Each and every one of us is *the one.*

> *Each of us is born with an inherent spiritual task. We have a sacred contract to use our own personal power wisely, responsively and lovingly.* 4
>
> ~ *Carolyn Myss*

When I first read- *We are the one's we've been waiting for,* I thought they were revolutionary. Yet, the more I thought about it the more I realized this statement is beyond revolutionary. It is *evolutionary.* Barack Obama was fully cognizant of their power when he spoke them on Super Tuesday.

Taking responsibility for our choices allows us to bear witness to the God given power each of us generates with every choice we make. We are as gods, so we might as well start acting like it.

There is a Hopi prophecy which proclaims: At the height of the white man's foolishness, great wisdom will return, if he listens, there will be a transformation of consciousness, if not, there will be cataclysmic disaster. Ram Dass adds, "If there ever was a time to wake up spiritually, this is it."5

The sooner we are willing to wake up and take full responsibility for the power of our free will, the sooner we will realize~

We Are the Ones We've Been Waiting For.

~

You could be a great horseman
and help free yourself and this world

though only if you and prayer become
sweet lovers.

It is a naïve man who thinks we are not
engaged in a fierce battle.

For I see and hear brave soldiers
all around me going mad,

falling on the ground in excruciating pain.

You could be a great horseman
and carry your heart through this world

like a life-giving sun,

though only if you and God become
sweet lovers. 6

~ Hafiz

Epilogue

I just had the following dream:

> I am working with a married man with a light spirit and curly, bright red hair. His wife arrives. Before leaving, he turns to caress my left breast. Then his wife begins stroking my left hip. Within moments eleven beaming blue eyed, red hair children with freckles are everywhere.

Could this be my Guardian Angel with his feminine counterpart and their offspring reappearing at the end of my book? I believe I have just been blessed body and soul.

While journaling my eyes fall upon a postcard on my dresser my daughter sent from the Louvre. It is Canova's sculpture of *Amor and Psyche* describing the love I feel flowing through me, expressing the union of human and divine.

Acknowledgements

I wish to express my deepest gratitude to each and everyone who supported me on this incredible journey.

To Sadie, Hannah, Avi, Shirah & Zev ~ for your love.

To Bonnie & Suzie~ for your honesty, love & support.

To Anne, Belinda, Joy, Tammy, Sandy & Susan~ for *being there* for me through thick & thin.

To Mark, Ollie, Theresa & Juliette my UK cheerleaders.

To Irene~ for introducing me to Jungian Psychology.

To Celia White~ for your firm, gentle editing.

To Micheal Morgulis~ for your vision & graphic design.

To Neshama Carlbach for letting me use your father's Rabbi Sholomo Carlbach (z'l) words as my title.

To Richard Wolin ~ for finding the missing piece.

To Franklin LaVoie~ for telling me to sit still & write.

To Morris Berman ~ for your inquiring mind.

To Trudy & Joy ~ for your valiant fourth quarter editing.

To everyone at RJ Communications ~ for helping me bring my dream into reality.

Notes

Preface

1. I first heard this prayer sung by Pir Vilayat Khan, head of the Sufi Order of the West. I later learned the melody was written by Rabbi Shlomo Carlebach.

Introduction

1. Rumi, transl. by Coleman Barks, *The Glance* (Penguin Books, 1999) p. 66.
2. Ram Dass, Mark Matousek & Marlene Roeder, Still Here (USA: Penguin Group, 2001)

Chapter 1 ~ Stepping Out

1. Hafiz, transl. Daniel Ladinsky, The Subject Tonight Is Love (New York: Penguin Compass, 2003) p. 55.
2. Eckhart Tolle, The Power of Now Calendar 2005.
3. Hafiz, transl. Daniel Ladinsky, The Gift (Arkana/ Penguin, 1999) p. 204.

Chapter 2 ~ Finding the Fountain of Life

1. Rumi (Tea Ceremony issue: Volume I, Number 2, 1996.)
2. *Look At A Fountain*. Rumi, transl. Coleman Barks, *Rumi: Bridge to the Soul*(Harper One, 2007) p.90.
3. Core Self Esteem. Steinem, Gloria. *Revolution From Within: A Book of Self Esteem*. (New York: Little Brown & Co., 1992.)
4. *For Three Days*. Hafiz, transl. Daniel Ladinsky, The Gift (Arkana/Penguin, 1999) p. Ibid. p. 295

Chapter 3 ~ Courage to Change the Things I Can

1. Serenity Prayer written by Reinhold Niebuhr in 1934.
2.. Bob Marley, *Redemption Song*.
3. Renate Craine, *Hidegard-Prophet of the Cosmic Christ*

(New York:The Crossroad Publishing Co. 1997.) p. 75.
4. Marianne Williamson. *A Woman's Worth* (New York: Random House, 1993.) p. 134.

Chapter 4 ~ Avoidance

1. Photos of tree and vortex by Theodor Schwenk, *Sensitive Chaos*. London: Rudolf Steiner Press, 1965.) pp. 34-5.
2. *The Pleiades*. Rumi, transl. by Coleman Barks, *The Glance* (Penguin Books, 1999) p. 20.
3. Dr. Suess *I had some trouble on the way to Solla Sollew.* (New York: Random House.)
4. Pierre Delattre, *Tales of the Dalai Lama* (Boston: Houghton Miffin, 1971)
5. *I Ching or Book of Changes, #5 Waiting/Nourishment* trans. Richard Wilhelm. (New Jersey: Princeton University Press , 1967) p. 24-5.

Chapter 5 ~ Hiding in Plain Sight

1. *Zikr*. Hafiz, transl. Daniel Ladinsky, The Gift(Arkana/ Penguin, 1999) p. Ibid. p. 244.

Chapter 6 ~ The Power of Love

1. Eckhart Tolle. *The Power of Now* (Namaste Publishing and New World Library, 1999)
2. Irene Claremont de Castillejo, *Knowing Woman* (Harper Colophon Books, 1973) pp. 134-8.
3. Julia Cameron *The Vein of Gold* (New York: Jeremy P. Tarcher/ Putnam Book,1996)
4. *Thunder Perfect Mind, Nag Hammadi* Elaine Pagels,*The Gnostic Gospels* (New York: Vintage Books, 1979), xvii, pp. 55-6.

Chapter 7~ Fixing What's Broken/ Tikkun Olam

1. Jesus, Gospel of Thomas. Elaine Pagels, *The Gnostic Gospels* (New York: Vintage Books,1979) p. 126.
2. Leloup, Jean-Yves, transl. by Joseph Rowe, *The Gospel of Mary Magdalene* (Inner Traditions, 2002)

pp.6, 37, 163.

How is it possible that the Teacher talked
In this manner, with a woman,
About secrets of which we ouraselves are ignorant?
Must we change our customs and listen to a woman?
Did he really choose her, and prefer her to us?
(Mary 17:9-20.)

Chapter 8 ~ Interfacing

1. . Leloup, Jean-Yves, transl. by Joseph Rowe, *The Gospel of Mary Magdalene* (Inner Traditions, 2002) p. 71.
2. Interview with Morris Berman by Barbara Goodrich-Dunn. (Common Boundary, July, August, 1991.)
3. Rainer Maria Rilke, transl. Stephen Mitchell. *Letters to a Young Poet* (New York: The Modern Library, 1984) pp. 34-5.
4. Neale Walsch, *Conversations with God* (New York: Putnam's Sons, 1995) p. 58.
5. Robert Bly, *The Little Book of the Human Shadow* (New York: Harper Collins Publication, 1982) pp. 15-27.
6. *Now Is The Time*. Hafiz, transl. Daniel Ladinsky, *The Gift* (Arkana/ Penguin, 1999) p. 160.
7. Joe Miller, as told to me Murshid Shahabuddin Less
8. Dr. Carl Jung, *Memoirs, Dreams, Reflections (*New York: Vintage Books,) p.302.

Chapter 9 ~ Reverberation

1. Vaclav Havel. *End of Communism is a serious warning to mankind. New York Times*, February 5, 1999.
2. Fritof Capra. *The Turning Point* (Bantam Books, 1982) pp. 80-81.
3. Chief Seattle Speech spoken in his native tongue. Transl. by Dr. Henry A. Smith in what is now Seattle in 1854. There is much controversy if Chief Seattle ever uttered these words.

Chapter 10 ~ The Orange Bird of Abundance

1. *It Felt Love*. Hafiz, trans. Daniel Ladinsky, *The Gift*

(Arkana/Penguin, 1999) p. 121.
2. Alice Walker, *The Color Purple* (A Harvest Book, Harcourt Inc. 1982) p. 103-4.
3. *The Thousand Stringed Instrument*. Hafiz, transl. Daniel Ladinsky, *The Gift* (Arkana/Penguin, 1999) p. 228.

Chapter 11 ~ Instant Karma

1. John Lennon with the Plastic Ono Band. *Instant Karma.* (Apple Records, 1970.)
2. . Leloup, Jean-Yves, transl. by Joseph Rowe, *The Gospel of Mary Magdalene* (Inner Traditions, 2002) pp. 58-9.
3. Ibid. p. 57.

Chapter 12 ~ The Red Earth Dream

1. Walter Kelley, *Pogo*. For 1st Earth Day poster, 1970.
2. SARK. *Succulent Wild Woman: Dancing with Your Wonder-Full Self. (New York: Simon & Shuster, 1997)*

Chapter 13 ~ Meetings with Remarkable Men

1. From the title of book and movie based on the life and spiritual search of G.I. Gurdjieff.
2. *No More Leaving*. Hafiz, transl. Daniel Ladinsky, *The Gift* (Arkana/Penguin, 1999) p. 258.
3. *Miles of Riverside Canbed.* Rumi, transl. Coleman Barks, *Rumi: Bridge to the Soul*(Harper One, 2007) p. 72-73.
4. *I Ching or Book of Changes, #5 Waiting/Nourishment* trans. Richard Wilhelm. (New Jersey: Princeton University Press , 1967) p. 24-5.
5. Hafiz, transl. by Daniel Ladinsky, *The Subject Tonight Is Love* (New York: Penguin Compass,2003) p.18.
6. Leloup, Jean-Yves, transl. by Joseph Rowe, *The Gospel of Mary Magdalene* (Inner Traditions, 2002) pp.61-2.

Chapter 14 ~ We Are the Ones We Have Been Waiting For

1. June Jordan, *Poems for South African Women* from *Passion: New Poems. 1977 -80.*
2. *Inside The Rose.* Rumi, transl. Coleman Barks, *Rumi*

Bridge to the Soul (Harper One, 2007) p.34-5.

3. Marianne Williamson, *Return to Love* (New York: Harper Collins, 1992.)
4. Carolyn Myss, *Anatomy of the Spirit.*(New York: Crown Publications, 1996) p. xi.
5. Dorothy Sisk & Paul Torrance, *Sprirtual Intelligence.* (Buffalo, New York: Creative Education Foundation Press, 2001) p. 137.
6. *Like a Life-Giving Sun.* Hafiz, transl. Daniel Ladinsky, *The Gift* (Arkana/Penguin, 1999) p. 28.

Bibliography

Arntz, W., B. Chase & M. Vincent, *What the Bleep Do We Know?*) Lord of the Wind, 2004.

Bly, Robert. *The Little Book of the Human Shadow* (New York: Harper Collins Publication, 1982)

Cameron, Julia. *The Vein of Gold* (New York: Jeremy P. Tarcher/ Putnam Book, 1996)

Castillejo, Irene Claremont de. *Knowing Woman* (Harper Colophon Books, 1973) pp. 134-8.

Chaung-tzu, F. Capra, *The Tao of Physics* (Boston: Shambala Press, 1975) p. 117

Capra, Fritof, *The Turning Point* (Bantam Books, 1982)

Cousens, Gabriel *Conscious Eating. (* Arizona: Essene Vision Books, 2000.)

Craine, Renate, *Hidegard-Prophet of the Cosmic Christ* (New York:The Crossroad Publishing Co. 1997.)

Delattre, Pierre. *Tales of the Dalai Lama* (Boston: Houghton Miffin, 1971)

Barbara Goodrich-Dunn. *Walking the Critical Path* (Common Boundary, July/ August, 1991.)

Hafiz, transl. Daniel Ladinsky, *The Gift* (Arkana/ Penguin, 1999)

---------*The Subject Tonight Is Love* (New York: Penguin Compass, 2003)

Havel, Vaclav. *End of Communism is a serious warning to mankind. New York Times*, February 5, 1999.

Jesus, Gospel of Thomas. Elaine Pagels, *The Gnostic Gospels* (New York: Vintage Books, 1979)

Jimenez, Juan Ramon, transl. Robert Bly. *News of the Universe* (Sierra Book Club) p.105.

Jordan, June. *Poems for South African Women* from *Passion: New Poems. 1977 -80.*

Jung, Dr. Carl. *Memoirs, Dreams, Reflections (*New York: Vintage Books.)

Lennon, John with the Plastic Ono Band. (Apple Records, 1970.)

McDuff, Shaun, Dean of Art Therapy, Leslie College.

Seen in Rowe Conference Center newsletter, 2008.

Myss, Carolyn, *Anatomy of the Spirit*.(New York: Crown Publications, 1996)

Ram Dass, Mark Matousek & Marlene Roeder, Still Here (USA: Penguin Group, 2001)

Rilke, Rainer Maria, transl. Stephen Mitchell. *Letters to a Young Poet*. (New York: The Modern Library, 1984)

Rumi, transl. by Coleman Barks, *The Glance* (Penguin Books, 1999)

—— *Rumi: Bridge to the Soul* (Harper One, 2007)

------- Rumi, Coleman Barks CD (Sounds True, 2002.

------- Rumi (Tea Ceremony issue: Volume I, Number 2, 1996.)

Sark. Julia Cameron, *The Vein of Gold* (New York: Jeremy P.Tarcher/ Putnam Book, 1996)

Schwenk, Theodor. *Sensitive Chaos*. London: Rudolf Steiner Press,1965.)

Sisk, Dorothy & Torrance, Paul. *Sprirtual Intelligence*. (Buffalo, New York: Creative Education Foundation Press, 2001)

Steinem, Gloria. *Revolution From Within: A Book of Self Esteem*. (New York: Little brown & Co., 1992.)

Suess, Dr. *I had some trouble on the way to Solla Sollew*. (New York: Random House.)

Tolle, Eckhart. *The Power of Now* (Namaste Publishing and New World Library, 1999)

Walker, Alice .*The Color Purple* (A Harvest Book, Harcourt Inc. 1982)

Walsch, Neale. *Conversations with God* (New York: Putnam's Sons, 1995)

Wilhelm, Richard. *The I Ching or Book of Changes* (New Jersey: Princeton University Press , 1967)

Williamson, Marianne. *Return to Love* (New York: Random House, 1992.)

------*A Woman's Worth* (New York: Random House, 1993.)

Index

Miriam's Drum Publications

Supports and Celebrates each person following their own path, finding their own truth and Returning to Self, Soul & God.

To arrange for Speaking Engagements, Group Readings & Book Signings with Miriam Minkoff or to purchase copies in bulk, visit
www.returntowhoyouare.com

Or write
Miriam's Drum Publications
373 Colvin Ave.
Buffalo, New York 14216